WHATSHISFACE

WHATSHISFACE

GORDON KORMAN

SCHOLASTIC INC.

The publisher does not have any control over and does not assume any responsibility for author or third-party websites or their content.

No part of this publication may be reproduced, stored in a retrieval system, or transmitted in any form or by any means, electronic, mechanical, photocopying, recording, or otherwise, without written permission of the publisher. For information regarding permission, write to Scholastic Inc., Attention: Permissions Department, 557 Broadway, New York, NY 10012.

This book is a work of fiction. Names, characters, places, and incidents are either the product of the author's imagination or are used fictitiously, and any resemblance to actual persons, living or dead, business establishments, events, or locales is entirely coincidental.

ISBN 978-1-338-20018-8

10 9 8 7 6 5 4 3   19 20 21 22 23

Printed in the U.S.A.   40

This book was originally published in hardcover by Scholastic Press in 2018. This edition first printing 2019

Book design by Baily Crawford

FOR MICHAEL AND TRUDY ISERSON,
IN-LAWS AND FRIENDS

CHAPTER ONE
MEET WHATSHISFACE

Cooper Vega is invisible.

Okay, not really. But when you're the new kid and people look right through you, it sure feels that way. Cooper is pretty much the world champion at being the new kid, since Stratford Middle is his fifth school in the past three years. He keeps his distance from the visible people on the soccer field to avoid being trampled by mistake. That's another thing about being invisible: It's your job to get out of the way.

At Stratford Middle School, the opposite of invisible is Brock Bumgartner. Right now, big Brock is poised in front of the goal, deflecting every ball that comes his way. He dives. He leaps. He flies. His hands are everywhere. He's just a blur. Nothing gets past him—especially not the compliments.

"Great save, Brock!"

"You're the man!"

"Best goalie in the state!"

Brock soaks up the praise for a while. He gets bored fast, though. "Come on, you guys. Let's play a game! The bell rings in fifteen minutes!"

They choose sides, but Brock's team ends up a man short. Many pairs of eyes scan the schoolyard, searching for an extra player.

Brock loses patience with this too. "Find somebody," he orders.

"What about Whatshisface over there?" suggests Aiden Scowcroft.

Cooper freezes. Aiden's long finger is pointing directly at him. This always comes sooner or later—the moment you become visible. Usually because they need something from you.

Brock turns around. "Whatshisface?" He looks right through Cooper.

"The new kid," Aiden persists. "The guy with the hair."

Cooper flinches, and his mop of shaggy brown hair— almost shoulder length—resettles itself. "My name is Cooper Vega," he supplies.

"All right, you're on defense," Brock tells him. "Don't mess up."

Eagerly, Cooper jogs onto the field. He's been a student at Stratford Middle School for a week and a half, and this is the first time anyone has noticed he's even alive. Changing schools every six months is standard stuff in the Vega family. Captain Vega's in the military. You go where you're sent and keep quiet about it. Cooper's used to the lifestyle, but that doesn't make it any easier. Especially in a town like

Stratford, where all the kids seem to have been together since they were old enough to walk. Cooper's happy to be included—even as Whatshisface or The New Kid. Some of the places he's been parachuted into have been welcoming and friendly. This isn't one of them.

Cooper isn't a stellar athlete to begin with, but he's especially awkward today. It's the phone—his brand-new GX-4000, the most advanced smartphone on the market. He's only had it since yesterday. It was his *sorry-we-had-to-move-you-away-from-all-your-friends-again* present. If he falls down and smashes it, he'll never forgive himself—and his parents will definitely never forgive him. The thing costs nearly twice as much as a top-of-the-line iPhone or Android. It's bigger and bulkier and feels somehow vulnerable in his pocket—like it's always on the verge of falling out.

"What are you doing, kid?" Brock's voice barks from behind Cooper. "You're just standing there! Get your head in the game!"

There's no question who the criticism is aimed at. The goalie has plenty of coaching for everybody, but all the others have names. Cooper is the only *kid*.

The shot comes out of nowhere—a booming kick on a laser trajectory at waist level. It's definitely a phone killer. As Cooper watches it approaching on a collision course with his front pocket, he understands that this is a choice between soccer glory and his GX-4000.

3

He makes the obvious choice. At the last second, he hurls his body out of the path of the ball, which sizzles past a flat-footed Brock into the net. The star goalie just stands there, openmouthed.

"New teams!" Brock bawls. "I'm not playing with Whatshisface!"

"We don't want him either!" is the reply from the opposite side of the field.

"Then get me another defender. I'll take anybody. Jolie—play defense. I don't care if you're a girl. You've got to be better than Whatshisface!"

Cooper slinks off the field. It's bad enough to be humiliated, but why does it have to be in front of Jolie Solomon, who's been the one bright spot in this miserable school? It would be an *honor* to be called Whatshisface by Jolie, who has never before glanced in Cooper's general direction. She's noticing him *now*—as the guy who made a fool of himself in a recess soccer game.

Jolie raises her arm, indicating a short cast around her wrist. "Can't. The cast doesn't come off till Thursday." Then, much to Cooper's surprise, she adds disapprovingly, "And his name *isn't* Whatshisface! It's—" She regards him in sudden surprise. "Sorry, I guess I never knew your name."

"Cooper," he tells her, following her off the field. "Cooper Vega."

"Cooper, Cooper, party pooper," calls a voice behind him.

"This is just great," Brock complains. "Where are we going to find another player in—what—seven minutes?"

Cooper looks worried, but Jolie is serene. "Don't let them get to you," she advises. "They're harmless. They just take their sports way too seriously. Especially Brock."

"You seem pretty sporty," Cooper observes, nodding toward her cast.

She shrugs. "Soccer's a little slow for me. I like to get the blood pumping. I broke my wrist kiteboarding on Lake Stratford."

"Kiteboarding?"

"You know—it's a cross between parasailing and water skiing, with a little snowboard thrown in. It's amazing how hard water is when you come down on it from thirty feet."

Cooper sizes up his companion. She's slim and kind of petite. Definitely not muscle-bound, or anything you would expect from an extreme athlete—not that he's met a lot of extreme athletes. Her T-shirt *does* say SCUBA INSANITY, with a cartoon of a diver taking an underwater selfie with a giant squid.

"You dive too?" he asks.

"Not that much anymore," she replies. "My dad won't let me go in where there are sharks. He's so overprotective. I also rock climb, zip-line, ski jump, bungee, and do parkour. I'll try normal things too—roller coasters aren't that boring, so long as they're really vertical. I'm also into drama. I want to be an actress when I grow up. Either that or an astronaut."

For Cooper, it's almost as bad as getting thrown out of the soccer game to find out how little he has in common with this girl.

"We just moved here three weeks ago," he says to keep the conversation going. "My dad's military. He's stationed at Fort Bensonhurst."

Jolie points off in the distance. "You can just make out the tower from here. Over there—in between those two hills. Our school is built on top of the third hill, so you can see for miles around. There should be a good spot to BASE jump around here, but believe me, I've checked. Nothing."

Cooper is shocked. "But you wouldn't actually do that, right?"

"I wish. My parents won't let me have a parachute till I'm eighteen. What's the point of living in Three Hills if you can't use the altitude?"

"Three Hills?" Cooper repeats.

"That used to be what the town was called—you know, before The Wolf moved in."

Cooper laughs. "Now you've really got me confused. Who's The Wolf?"

"Somerset Wolfson—one of the richest men in America. Surely you've noticed his estate? His mansion is the biggest building in town." She walks him to the south side of the playground. "See all that? Every inch of it is his. That's the house. And that other building is the museum."

Cooper gazes out over the vast property, which seems to take up the entire south end of town. It looks like a national park, with gleaming marble buildings, rolling lawns, glittering ponds, sumptuous flower beds, and handsome groves of trees.

No question: This is a man with a *ton* of money.

"Why does he have his own museum?" Cooper asks.

"He's a Shakespeare nut," Jolie explains. "He has the biggest private collection in the world. That's the only reason he moved here thirty years ago—he needed a good spot to put up a custom-made gallery for all the old books and documents and artifacts. Everything is so old that it has to go in special climate-controlled cases. Plus, he needs security. It's worth so much money that even a billionaire can't afford to lose it."

Upon closer inspection, Cooper can see that the greenery has been strategically placed to hide a heavy stone wall and a high security gate.

"Mr. Wolfson must really love Shakespeare," he comments.

"Tell me about it! Back in the day, he refused to buy the property unless Three Hills agreed to change its name to Stratford—that was Shakespeare's hometown in England. It was hard times back when he made the offer, and the town needed the cash, so they agreed. My parents remember it. It was a huge deal for the locals. A lot of people are still ticked off at The Wolf for using his money to push us around."

Cooper takes his new phone out of his pocket and begins tapping at the screen, searching for the camera app. He's still getting used to its practically countless functions.

Jolie is impressed. "Wow, is that a GX-4000? I've heard about them, but I've never seen one."

"It's the latest bribe," he tells her. "Every time we have to move, my parents get my sister and me something great to make up for it." He frames a panoramic shot of the mansion and museum. "Something to send my friends back in Colorado." As he reaches to take the picture, the image on the screen dissolves into multicolored snow. There's an angry tone, and the phone powers itself off.

"Oops," Cooper says, embarrassed. "I'm new at this. I must have zigged when I should have zagged."

"My phone is kind of buggy too," Jolie says sympathetically. "Of course, that might be from the time it fell out of my pocket on top of that rock-climbing wall. But it works—sometimes."

"Mine's brand-new, so it should work all the time." The GX-4000 powers up again with a series of beeps and an odd whistling that sounds like nothing Cooper's ever heard coming from an electronic device. He points the lens at the Wolfson property.

"Wait!" Jolie leans into the frame, beaming and holding up two V-for-victory signs.

Okay, she's blocking the museum and at least half of the mansion, but who cares about that? For a picture of Stratford to send to the old neighborhood, this is perfect. Maybe the guys will think she's his girlfriend. What do they know? They're in Colorado.

He takes the shot. A faint blue spark jumps from the screen to his finger.

"Ow!" The phone drops from his hand onto the grass.

"Wow," Jolie comments. "Your phone really *is* buggier than mine."

Cooper stoops to pick it up. "No problem. It's all in one piece. Now, this time, if you stand a little to the left—"

He's interrupted by the school bell.

"Gotta go. See you in class." She joins the stampede for the building.

Cooper hangs back, scrolling through pages of unfamiliar apps in search of the photo library. One entry, it says.

Well, what do you know? he thinks. *This overpriced, overcomplicated gizmo actually took a real picture.*

He taps the icon and examines it. There are the other two hills in the distance, the sprawling Wolfson place in front of them. And there's Jolie—her outline, anyway. You can see her arms and the two V-for-victory signs. But the rest of her is hidden behind a silver-gray shimmer of distortion right in the middle of the photograph. It might as well be a picture of Godzilla—if Godzilla had fingers.

Of course. The phone you get for ninety-nine cents at Walmart takes pictures just fine, but this magnificent piece of technology sticks a silver blob in front of the only part of the photograph that's worth taking.

The second bell rings—the late one. Not only is he Whatshisface; he's on the verge of becoming Whatshisface with a detention.

Cooper stuffs the phone back in his pocket and runs to join the last of the stragglers at the door.

As a military kid, he's gotten used to a lot of towns—some good, some bad, some in between. But this place gives him an uneasy feeling.

CHAPTER TWO

SMARTPHONE, STUPID PERSON

Veronica Vega has a new boyfriend. Already. Chad Bumgartner—Brock's sixteen-year-old brother.

Three weeks in this town, and it's like Veronica was born here. She has a happening social life, a boyfriend; she's on the volleyball team, the pep squad, the yearbook staff. The whole high school might as well just shut down if she moves away. Which she probably will, and sooner rather than later, the way their dad keeps getting transferred.

It's always that way. Veronica's a perfect fit wherever she goes, while her brother remains Whatshisface. She also has a phone that works. It's identical to Cooper's, another GX-4000, with a serial number only one away from his, proving that they came off the assembly line side by side.

That's where the similarity ends.

"It shoots the most awesome video," she raves at the dinner table. "Even in low light. You should see the amazing footage I took of the bonfire at the lake last night. It's so sharp."

"I don't think mine's that good," Cooper says. "It makes a lot of weird noises—beeps and clicks and honks."

"You're just not used to it yet," Captain Vega reassures him. "Remember, it's top-of-the-line technology, real cutting edge. Those must be notifications. Once you're familiar with all its capabilities, the different sounds will make sense to you."

"They aren't normal phone sounds. Remember that house we lived in where the wind used to whistle through our chimney? I can't remember which town it was. Anyway, that's what it makes."

"I think it was Dover," Mrs. Vega muses. "But I'm sure you're imagining things, Coop. No phone sounds like wind in a chimney."

"This one does," Cooper insists. "And there's something wrong with the camera. All the pictures are blurry."

"It must be you," his sister informs him. "My pictures are amazing. You're just messing up the focus."

"That doesn't explain the silver stuff. Where does that come from?"

She shrugs. "What do you expect when you give a smartphone to a stupid person?"

"Veronica," their mother puts in disapprovingly. "Your brother's younger than you. He has to learn the operating system at his own pace."

"Look!" Cooper exclaims. He places his phone at the center of the table and scrolls through his pictures—the view from his bedroom window; the family SUV; Melrose, the next-door neighbors' black Lab, lounging on the grass. Each one marred by the same silvery blur. "What's that, huh?"

"Sun glare," Captain Vega concludes. "Our engineers have the same problem in the military. Our targeting systems have to be able to tell the difference between what's real and what isn't."

The phone emits a mournful whistle as the image of Melrose dissolves into static.

Mrs. Vega frowns. "That actually *does* remind me of our old chimney. Yes, Delaware. Definitely."

"It has to be some kind of alert," Veronica decides. "Check your settings to see if there's a software update available."

"The last time I did that, it shocked me," Cooper complains.

That night, while Captain Vega spends three hours on the phone with tech support, Cooper sneaks into his sister's room and examines her GX-4000. She's right. The thing works like a charm. It doesn't beep or chime or honk unless there's a message coming in. The pictures boast vivid colors and sharp detail. Most of these are of Chad Bumgartner, who looks like an older, more muscled clone of Brock—the same fair skin, thick neck, and concrete flattop haircut.

Finally, Captain Vega finishes with tech support. "We did a full diagnostic," he tells Cooper, handing back the device. "Everything checks out."

Later, Cooper lies awake in bed, tossing and turning while the GX-4000 sits on the nightstand, chirping and whistling. It sounds like R2-D2 in an echo chamber or on the edge of the Grand Canyon.

There's an angry pounding on the wall. Veronica's voice comes from the next room: "Quit playing with your phone! Some of us are trying to sleep!"

"I'm not playing with it!" Cooper calls back. "I'm not even touching it. It's doing all that on its own."

"Put it on silent," she growls through the wall. "Better still, shut it down."

"Fine." Cooper holds the power button. The home screen hangs on a lot longer than it should as the grid of apps flickers and the icons begin to spin.

Hmmm, that's new. He watches as the apps dissolve into snow. It's a clockwise swirl that reminds him of a flushing toilet. The multicolored particles begin to collect in the vortex, where the drain would be. But instead of being swallowed up, the points of light gather in the center of the screen, forming a shape that ripples and undulates. It continues to grow, a spreading amoeba. No, wait—that's no amoeba. A head . . . two arms . . . two legs . . .

A *person?*

Then the monitor goes black. The GX-4000 is finally off.

It vibrates intermittently all night, before powering up again all on its own a little before dawn.

*   *   *

That morning, Cooper practically sleepwalks to school. Just about the only thing keeping him awake is the phone in his back pocket, buzzing and chiming. He barely slept, thanks to the GX-4000. Even when the thing was still, he was wound up tight as a drum, waiting for the next explosion to send it vibrating across the nightstand. It was like that water torture that drives you insane waiting for the next drop.

"Hi, Cooper!"

He's struggling along, his eyes half-closed, so when he spots Jolie, he thinks he's hallucinating. She's bobbing up and down like she's on a trampoline. In amazement, he realizes she's riding a pogo stick, hopping along the sidewalk in the direction of Stratford Middle School.

She comes alongside him, bouncing in place. "Great way to travel, huh? Good exercise too." She isn't even breathing hard.

"I guess you're really into physical fitness," he offers. The effort of maintaining eye contact is making him seasick.

"My two careers, remember? Actress and astronaut. You have to be in shape for both of them. You're trying out for the play, right?"

"Play?" Why is he always so clueless around her?

"Yeah. *Romeo and Juliet.* The seventh grade does a Shakespeare play every year—part of the whole Stratford thing. Personally, I'd rather do a musical, like *Annie* or *Phantom of the Opera*, but The Wolf pays for the sets and costumes, so it's Shakespeare twenty-four/seven. Anyway, it has to be better than what last year's seventh graders got. People around here still call it *Macdeath*."

"Yeah, that must have been a downer," Cooper agrees.

She hops off the pogo stick and holds it out to him. "Want to try?"

Cooper knows he shouldn't. He's too tired, and—let's face it—not the most coordinated kid in the world besides. But there's something about Jolie that makes him want to please her, to share her interests. And as unstable as that pogo stick looks, it has to be safer than her other hobbies, like scuba diving with sharks. If she invites him to join her at that, he's definitely going to have to say no.

Gingerly, he accepts the stick and climbs onto the foot bar, moving very tentatively, testing his balance.

"It's easy, right?" she prompts.

"Right—easy." It's not easy at all. The bouncing part isn't so bad; it's the not-falling that's just about impossible. Every hop has him keeling over in one direction or another, hanging on in white-knuckled terror.

"Hey!" booms a deep voice. "Check out Whatshisface!"

Cooper twirls around in time to see Brock and a couple of his soccer friends pointing and laughing. The spring end comes down in a crack in the sidewalk, and the pogo stick is launched like a missile. With a cry of shock, Cooper is tossed into a hedge. The last thing he sees before hitting the scratchy branches is his phone flying out of his pocket.

The screen of the GX-4000 lights up in midair, and when it strikes the pavement, the click of the camera sounds. Cooper struggles out of the bushes to behold an amazing sight. Rising from his phone is a silver cloud, luminous and transparent.

He's thunderstruck. The camera isn't broken at all. The reason his pictures are marred by a silvery shimmer is that the silvery shimmer is *real*!

"Did you see that?" he blurts.

"See it?" Brock exclaims. "I wish I had it on video! Greatest wipeout ever!"

"Nine point five," Aiden adds. "You only lost marks because you didn't split your head open."

"No! I mean—" Cooper points to the glittering shape over the phone and realizes that it's no longer there.

Jolie is rescuing her pogo stick from the tangle of the hedge, and Brock and his friends are high-fiving in honor of Cooper's performance. No one else noticed the fleeting image.

Jolie holds out the pogo stick. "Want to get right back on the horse?"

"That's okay," Cooper tells her. "I should probably run home and wash out some of these cuts before school. You know, maybe get some Band-Aids."

"Good idea," Brock approves. "No sense bleeding all over everybody. You can walk with us, Jolie. Or bounce, or whatever you do on that thing."

"*If* you guys think you can keep up." Jolie gets back on the pogo stick and springs off in the direction of school. By the time she gets up to speed, Brock and company have to run to keep pace with her.

Cooper barely notices their departure or the pain of the many scratches all over his body. The memory of the shimmering form over the fallen GX-4000 stays with him. No way this is just buggy technology. This is something he can *see*!

What is it? A cloud, sure, but a cloud of *what*? He allows the image to re-form in his mind's eye. The problem with clouds is that if you stare at them long enough, all sorts of things begin to appear. It comes more from your imagination than anything that's actually there.

Yet the more he visualizes the glistening shape, the more he realizes he's seen it before. It was on the GX-4000's screen when he tried to shut it off last night, formed by the swirling particles right before the monitor finally went dark.

A head. Arms. Legs. A body.

A person.

CHAPTER THREE
SHAKESPEARE TOWN

Auditions for *Romeo and Juliet* are held at lunch that day. It isn't exactly mandatory to try out, but all seventh graders are assigned an eating time and an auditioning time—the message being that the two activities are equal in importance. If there was a breathing time, Cooper decides, it would probably come in third.

Mr. Marchese, his homeroom teacher, is the play's director. He seems horrified at the suggestion that maybe Cooper wants to give this year's production a pass.

"Of course you want to be a part of it!" the teacher says. "Why wouldn't you?"

"Well, I'm kind of still the new guy," Cooper explains. "Nobody really knows me."

"All the more reason why you should *participate*." When Mr. Marchese says *participate*, it's with a thrill in his voice, as if he's tasting something really delicious and trying to make the experience last. "This is the Shakespeare town. What better way to fit in and make friends than to put yourself where you'll be working shoulder to shoulder with every other kid your age in Stratford? Ask the eighth graders. They had a blast last year!"

"You mean with *Macdeath*?"

Mr. Marchese smiles. "Okay, *Macbeth* might have been a little heavy for middle school. But the year before that, *A Midsummer Night's Dream* was great. Kids in fairy wings all over the stage, and then Keith Aberfeldy had an asthma attack inside that donkey head, but he fought through it and saved the performance! He's considered a hero today. None of the cast will ever forget it. If you don't want to be an actor, at least join the crew. Paint scenery. Work the lights. *Something.*"

In the cafeteria, there's no mistaking the buzz of anticipation. Every few minutes, another group of seventh graders bus their trays and head off to the gym, where the auditions are taking place. The eighth graders are reminiscing about the good old days, when it was their turn, and the sixth graders are talking about next year.

At twelve forty, Cooper presents himself at the gym with a crew of classmates that includes Jolie, Aiden, and Brock.

"I didn't practice," he says nervously as they wait on the bench.

Brock snorts a laugh. "There's nothing to practice, kid. They just give you some lines and you read them. That's it."

"His name is Cooper, not *kid*," Jolie tells Brock. "And for your information, I've been studying the play since last summer. I know all Juliet's lines by heart—that's the part I'm hoping for."

"You wasted your time," Aiden informs her. "You're going to be Juliet whether you prepared for it or not. Who else are they going to give it to?"

"Your name's practically Juliet already," Brock adds. "Switch up a couple of letters and you're done."

Jolie glows, and Cooper wishes he'd had the brains to say that. He has to admit she looks like the ultimate Juliet—even in a SKI EVEREST T-shirt, which they probably didn't have in Shakespeare's time.

Lamar Dingle is currently in the hot seat, reading from a card. He's doing a pretty good job, from what Cooper can tell. Not that much of the flowery language makes any sense to him:

> *"What light through yonder window breaks?*
> *It is the east, and Juliet is the sun . . ."*

"I thought Juliet was a girl," Aiden comments, frowning.

"She's faking it" is Brock's explanation. "You know, pretending to be some guy's son so she won't get blamed for the broken window."

Cooper is pretty sure that's wrong, but he doesn't have a story to replace it, so he keeps his mouth shut.

"Romeo is so in love with Juliet that he compares her to a rising sun," Jolie whispers. "Jeez, guys, how dense can you get?"

Cooper snickers, but he's becoming aware of a new problem. His phone is beginning to vibrate in his pocket. That wouldn't be too surprising if it was set on vibrate. But it's 100 percent off—at least it was when Cooper entered the school building that morning. How can he take it out to see what's up with it without waving it in front of the seventh-grade teachers?

A few more kids read from different parts of the play. In order to get a little more oomph into the auditions, Mr. Marchese tries to convince everyone that Shakespeare's rhyming couplets are no different from rap songs. The Bard, he argues, was actually the world's first hip-hop mogul. Maybe so, Cooper notes, but there aren't a lot of rap songs with *forsooth* or *methinks* in them.

The performances don't change much. A lot of the kids are terrible. Amazingly, Brock turns out to be pretty good— not because he knows anything about acting or Shakespeare, but thanks to his loud voice and cocky confidence. Brock believes everything he says because it's coming out of his royal mouth. Aiden, on the other hand, can barely mumble loud enough to be heard.

Next it's Jolie's turn. Mr. Marchese holds out a card with some lines on it. Jolie glances at it briefly and waves it away. Then she turns toward the nervously milling seventh graders and speaks in a voice rich with feeling and clear as a bell:

> "O Romeo, Romeo! Wherefore art thou, Romeo?
> Deny thy father and refuse thy name.
> Or, if thou wilt not, be but sworn my love . . ."

"Shakespeare's such a rip-off," Aiden puts in sourly. "They always talk about swearing, but you never get so much as a single curse word."

Cooper ignores him, so wrapped up is he in Jolie's performance. It's not the words, which are so alien that they might as well be in a foreign language. It's the intensity of her voice, the passion of her acting. She *becomes* Juliet, and Cooper can feel her love for Romeo, even though the lines she's reading are hundreds of years old, and part of a play he barely understands. He's electrified—and for sure his phone is. The device is going crazy in his pocket.

Maybe it's just Cooper, but he can't shake the feeling that she's making this speech to him and him only.

"Check out Whatshisface," Brock comments. "Methinks he's in love or something."

"Hey—" Cooper wants to present a stronger defense, but there really is something wrong with the GX-4000. No way is this normal vibration. It feels like a jackhammer against his hip.

Jolie's still performing, even though she has to be well past the selection on the card. Mr. Marchese doesn't stop her. He's watching with delighted admiration. The entire gym is enraptured.

All at once, an earsplitting *blurp* explodes out of Cooper's pocket. It sounds like a speeding fire truck warning traffic and pedestrians out of the way. Everyone jumps, including Jolie, who ends her audition to scattered applause.

Mr. Marchese is furious. "Who did that? Was that a *phone?*"

Cooper jams his hand in his pocket to turn off the GX-4000. It's supposed to be off already! As soon as he finds the power button, he receives an electric shock that travels from his finger all the way down to his toes.

Brock is snickering at him. "Methinks it's Whatshisface," he hisses to Aiden.

"Forsooth, me agrees," says Aiden with a grin.

Mr. Marchese sighs. "Thanks, Jolie. That was fantastic. Let's move on. Our last audition this period is"—he consults his clipboard—"Cooper Vega."

Cooper is so used to being Whatshisface that he almost doesn't answer to his own name.

Jolie whispers an encouraging "You're going to be great!" as they pass on the apron of the stage. Cooper scans the lines on the card the director gives him—something about being "fortune's fool." The instant he whispers the words to himself, the phone on his hip starts up again. This time the buzzing works in a circular pattern that tickles, and he blunders his way through the audition wriggling and giggling like a complete idiot.

"Thank you, Cooper. That was—uh—very good."

The director doesn't seem angry. His emotion seems closer to pity.

Cooper pities himself. If there was ever any chance of being Romeo to Jolie's Juliet, he's just fumbled it away, thanks to the GX-4000.

He exits the gym to a chorus of smothered laughter and a few not-so-quiet jeers.

Jolie calls, "Nice job, Cooper."

That hurts even more than the rest of it because it's so obviously not true.

Out in the hall, away from prying eyes, he checks his phone to see how many hours are left in this miserable day. But before he can see the time, the GX-4000 powers off and sits idle in his palm, quiet and harmless.

CHAPTER FOUR
WRONG NUMBER?

The ramp is pointed more or less in the direction of the moon.

The rider comes hurtling down the hill on a BMX bike, picking up speed with every yard of pavement. The only way to tell it's Jolie is that the video is posted on her Instagram account. Her face is hidden behind a helmet and a mirrored visor.

By the time she hits the ramp, she's just a blur. She rockets up the slope and then she's airborne, heaving the front wheel of the bike high. Cooper is terrified for her, even though he knows she's alive, because he just saw her at school today. And yet the stunt is so dangerous that it doesn't seem possible any human being could survive it.

Halfway to the ionosphere, the bike begins its descent. It's a long way down. Even though Cooper can't see her face, Jolie's body language makes it clear that she's enjoying every millisecond, drinking it in, reveling in it. It's a perfect landing on the rear wheel—or at least it is for the first couple of heartbeats. But the bike is moving too fast and she can't control it. A wobble in the front tire and it's all over. The wipeout is as spectacular as the jump itself. And the most amazing part of all? The pure joy as she throws off her helmet and leaps to her feet, clutching at what turns out to be the broken wrist that hasn't completely healed yet.

Cooper can't look away. She may be 80 percent bananas, but she's the most incredible person he's ever met. And when he scrolls down the Instagram feed, another video starts up, with a stunt that's even more guaranteed to maim and kill. This time she's bundled in Gore-Tex with crampons on her feet, making her way up a frozen waterfall, wielding two ice axes. Over her shoulder, a fat sun is rising, but its orange brilliance pales next to the sheer bliss on her face. She loves this as much as Cooper would hate it.

"It is the east," he mumbles aloud, remembering the auditions, "and Jolie is the sun."

All at once, the GX-4000 emits a sound like a truck with bad brakes and vibrates its way out of his hand, dropping to the carpeted floor. By the time Cooper stoops to pick it up, the image on the screen has dissolved into a whirlwind of particles.

"Not again." The phone is dark, but after a few seconds, it lights back up, the screen dancing with color, morphing in and out of elusive shapes.

Then the GX-4000 does something new and unexpected. It *speaks*.

"Is anyone there?"

Cooper freezes. What now? Is someone Skyping him? Video chatting? Nothing rang, and Cooper never answered any call.

He says the first thing that comes to mind, not realizing how stupid it sounds until the words are already out. "I think you have the wrong number."

"Number?" the voice asks. "Who speaketh thus?"

Cooper frowns. Someone is crank calling him—probably Brock or Aiden or one of those jerks, putting on a fancy British accent and talking like Shakespeare. They're trying to make him look even stupider than he looked at the audition.

"*I* speaketh thus!" Cooper growls. "How did you get this number?"

"Show thyself, stranger, that I might look upon thee."

"Now, listen, you—"

Cooper's breath catches in his throat. He watches dumbstruck as the swirling snow on the screen slowly collects in the center.

A man—no, a kid. A boy not much older than Cooper.

But this is no ordinary kid. He looks—wrong. He wears a dingy white shirt with puffy sleeves, patched at the elbows and held in place by a tight-fitting vest laced down to his waist. His hair is a mass of fair curls topped by a strange hat—almost like a baseball cap with no brim, only softer, velvety. Instead of pants, he wears what look like bloomers that end midthigh. His legs are clad in tights. His shoes are more like slippers, made of some kind of soft leather.

"What are you supposed to be—Robin Hood?" Cooper asks.

The boy is clearly annoyed. "Waste not my time with thy silly jests! I demand to know the nature of this place!"

"Hey, hey, back up!" Cooper retorts. "You called me, remember?"

"You would have done the same," the boy states firmly. "So long in darkness, surrounded by this featureless ether. So many unfamiliar sounds, nearby yet unseen. And then a window opens and I behold thee. A stranger sight these eyes have never seen."

"*I'm* strange? Hath you looked in the mirror lately? I'm hanging up now!" Cooper taps the phone, but the end-call option does not appear. This isn't Skype or any app like that. Come to think of it, in order for this kid's whole body to be on-screen, he has to be standing at least ten feet away from his phone or computer, or whatever he's calling on. In that case, though, wouldn't Cooper be able to see the room around him?

The stranger is totally visible, from the string that ties his collarless shirt at his throat to the stripes on his pantaloons. But there's nothing around him—not a lamp, not a table, not a picture on a wall, or even a wall itself.

Cooper thinks of the boy's words—*featureless ether*. This is no crank call, and this kid is no dimwit like Brock, putting on his Halloween costume to pull Whatshisface's chain. The person on the screen seems to be telling the *truth*—or at least the truth as he understands it.

Of all the messed-up things the GX-4000 has done, this one is top of the list.

Cooper asks the million-dollar question: "Who are you?"

"Roderick Barnabas Northrop, printer's apprentice. Thou mayest call me Roddy, if it pleaseth thee. And thou art . . . ?"

"Cooper Vega. Uh—seventh grader."

"The seventh grade of what?" Roddy inquires. "What is thy apprenticeship?"

"I'm not an apprentice. I'm in middle school."

Roddy's brow furrows under his fringe of curls. "Thy words are peculiar to mine ears. As I suspect my words are to thine."

Cooper sighs. "Tell me about it."

"I have just done thus," Roddy says in surprise. "Thy manner of speaking is unusual. What part of England art thou from?"

"No part of England," Cooper replies. "I'm an American."

Roddy's eyes open wide. "The Americas—the New World! How is it that I can see thee? What is this miracle?"

Cooper's head has been spinning throughout this impossible encounter. He knows he has to ground himself—find some connection between this weirdness and reality. When the next question forms on his tongue, he realizes it's the one he should have asked first.

"Roddy—what year is this?"

Roddy answers immediately. "Why, it is the year of our Lord 1596, of course."

"No way!" Cooper blurts. "It's 2018!"

"Dost thou think me an idiot?"

"Look!" Cooper holds the phone screen up to the school calendar hanging on his wall.

"September 2018!" Roddy reads the date in astonishment. "What is this deceit? What harm have I done thee that I am treated thus?"

"It's the truth! You think I printed up a fake calendar on the off chance that some weirdo from 1596 might show up on my phone?"

"I know not this 'phone'!" Roddy tells him in growing agitation. "Explain thyself!"

"It's this, uh, machine I carry around." Cooper struggles to find words that might make sense to Roddy. "Everybody has phones in 2018. You talk to people on them—that's how I'm talking to you right now. And I can see you—I mean, not the real you. More like your *image*."

"Impossible," Roddy declares firmly. "I have never sat for any portrait."

"It's not the same thing. There's a camera—" He cuts off the explanation. If you've never heard of a phone, you probably don't know what a camera is either.

There's a knock at the door, and Mrs. Vega leans into the room. "It's getting kind of late, Coop. Don't you think you can talk to your friend tomorrow?"

Cooper quickly places the GX-4000 facedown on his bedspread. "Okay, Mom," he mumbles, not at all sure if there will be a tomorrow with this particular "friend." He isn't totally convinced it's happening now.

"All right, honey, sleep well."

Cooper waits until her footsteps recede down the hall before turning the phone over again. "Sorry, that was just my mom—"

He's talking to a blank screen. "You can come out now, Roddy. The coast is clear." He tries again. "Uh—thy coast is clearest." Nothing.

He presses the home button, but the only thing to appear is the array of apps.

He speaks into the voice command. "Dial the most recent caller."

The number that appears on the screen is his mom's. Cooper hangs up, determined to reach Roddy again. But how? As far as Cooper knows, Roddy doesn't have a phone number. He doesn't even understand what a phone is. How do you dial into the past? Long distance? How about long ago?

Feeling foolish, Cooper brings up the keypad and taps in 1-5-9-6.

"Your call cannot be completed as dialed . . ."

Cooper knows it can't. The question is: How was it completed the first time around?

He lies on his back, staring at the darkened phone. How many hours has he spent over the past few days trying to will this miserable piece of junk to shut up, to cut out the blurping, buzzing, chiming, and vibrating that keep him up night after night? Well, now he has his wish. The thing is totally quiet. Somehow, though, he understands that he'll get even less sleep tonight, tossing and turning, wondering if he's losing his mind.

Did he really just have a conversation with a kid who lived hundreds of years ago? How? Buggy phones are pretty common. They'll definitely drive you nuts. What they won't do is communicate with past centuries.

And yet there's the evidence of Cooper's own eyes and ears. Roddy—the things he said and the way he said them. The accent. The words that sound like Shakespeare's plays. Even Roddy's strange clothing seems familiar, as if Cooper has seen it before. And he has—when Mr. Marchese showed everybody the school's wardrobe room on audition day.

Or did I hallucinate the whole thing?

That's possible too. In fact, it's probably true.

The longer he lies awake, waiting for his dormant phone

to burst to life, the more convinced he becomes that the entire "conversation" was a figment of his imagination, the result of a stressful move to a town full of jerks. Plus, he has Shakespeare on the brain, thanks to *Romeo and Juliet*.

He changes into pajamas and climbs into bed. It's settled, then. There's no Roddy Northrop, and there never was.

Cooper pulls the covers to his chin. That solves one problem and opens up another.

The fact that I'm probably going crazy.

CHAPTER FIVE
THE GHOST IN THE MACHINE

"Somerset Wolfson made his billions in chromite exploration in the Ring of Fire region of the Canadian far north," Mr. Marchese is explaining. "But his passion has always been Shakespeare. He acted in the plays as a college student, and later in life began collecting rare folios of the Bard's works. When he retired, he built a museum so he could share his love of Shakespeare with the world—Cooper, are we keeping you up?"

The teacher's voice snaps Cooper out of a light doze. "I'm listening!" he blurts. He almost is, but a sleepless night stressing over the strange encounter on his phone—which may or may not have really happened—has left him exhausted. "You're talking about when The Wolf moved here and got everybody to change the town name to Stratford."

Mr. Marchese smiles. "I know you're new. But around here, we try not to refer to the man who put our community on the map as The Wolf."

Cooper feels a spitball ricochet off the back of his neck. "Way to disrespect our town!" hisses a voice he's pretty sure belongs to Brock.

"Sorry," Cooper mumbles, his face burning.

"We'll all have a chance to tour Mr. Wolfson's collection in a few weeks," the teacher continues. "Every year, the seventh grade takes a field trip to the museum before the show. It's a pretty moving experience, especially since we'll be just about ready to perform our *Romeo and Juliet.*"

Cooper sits up a little straighter and tries to pay attention as Mr. Marchese goes on about the Wolfson Collection. In addition to the very earliest editions of Shakespeare's plays dating back centuries, there are displays of clothing, tools, and illustrations from Elizabethan England, the time of Shakespeare. There's a detailed replica of the Globe Theatre, where many of the plays were originally performed. There are even rumors that not all of Mr. Wolfson's collection is on display. Around Stratford, the word is that the billionaire is keeping a secret gallery filled with Shakespearean artifacts no one has ever seen. It's impossible to guess what these objects might be, but everyone assumes they were acquired illegally. Mr. Wolfson is a great man, but he'd stop at nothing to get his hands on an important piece of Shakespeare history.

Cooper feels his eyelids starting to droop. Yikes! If he falls asleep again, he'll never be able to bluff through it with Mr. Marchese.

That's when it happens. A distant voice calls, "Coopervega!"

Cooper's lolling head snaps to attention. "I'm awake!"

"So I see," Mr. Marchese tells him mildly. His eyes narrow. "Are you all right, Cooper?"

The voice comes again. "Coopervega!"

Cooper pivots in his chair, trying to see who's calling him. Brock? Aiden? Do those guys even know his name? To them, he's Whatshisface.

"I seek thee, Coopervega. Hast thou a place in this darkness?"

With a sinking heart, Cooper realizes that the muffled message is coming from his pocket, where the GX-4000 is vibrating.

Oh, no! *He's* back. Who else would use those words? That accent?

"I—I—have to go to the bathroom!"

Cooper is up and running for the door even before Mr. Marchese gives the okay. He darts down the hall, bursts into the boys' room, and hides himself in the far stall. "Roddy— Roddy, is that you?"

"'Tis I," comes the gloomy response. "But I see thee not."

Cooper whips out his phone and presses the home button. The boy from last night's "hallucination" is center screen, framed in murky shadow, round-shouldered with dejection, his face a picture of suffering.

"What's the matter?" Cooper asks anxiously.

The boy raises a limp hand to his brow. "I am dead, Coopervega. Coopervega, I am dead."

"No, you're not! I'm looking right at you."

Roddy shakes his head tragically. "I have recalled my final moment, retaken my final breath."

"You're just a kid!" Cooper protests.

"The plague knows neither age nor mercy."

"Plague?" Cooper echoes. "You mean *bubonic* plague?" He almost drops the phone, as if it might be contagious. "But— if you're dead . . . Roddy, are you saying you're a *ghost*?"

Roddy nods miserably. "Aye, a ghost. A spirit."

Cooper is stunned. How can this be happening? There's no such thing as ghosts! And even if there was, how did one get into his GX-4000?

"Well, at least now I know what's wrong with my phone," Cooper says in a shaky voice. "It isn't buggy. It's haunted."

"This 'phone' again. I understand it not." Roddy stretches out his arms. "I feel no machine around me."

Cooper swallows hard. "I hate to tell you this, but you might not have an actual body anymore. A phone's small enough to hold in your hand. It's for talking to people far away."

"To ghosts?"

"Um—alive people mostly," Cooper replies. "There are no ghosts—I mean, there *weren't.* You know—before you."

Roddy is distraught. "I am the *only one?*"

"Probably," Cooper tells him. "Maybe. You can't go by me. I don't believe in ghosts. At least, I *didn't.*"

"How can this be?" Roddy protests. "Thou art far in the future. All others of my time are surely as dead as I. And those from the ages before me, and many ages after. And I, the only ghost?"

Cooper shrugs. "I can't explain it either. Just lucky, I guess."

"Lucky," Roddy echoes, the word strange to him. "Oh, I am fortune's fool. Trapped and alone in this ether, surrounded by the blackest night, my only window the occasional glimpse of thee."

Fortune's fool. Cooper remembers the line from *Romeo and Juliet* for a second, then moves on. He has bigger things to worry about than any play. "What about me?" he complains. "No tech support's ever going to believe me when I tell them my phone has a ghost in it. They'll just say I'm crazy and I should download the latest software update."

"That does sound painful," Roddy sympathizes.

"It's not painful; it's just a pain. I know you've got problems too, Roddy, but I *need* my phone. The thing won't even take pictures without these weird cloudy shapes—"

Cooper frowns at the memory of the photographs he tried to take. Every one was spoiled by the same silvery distortion, that almost-human form . . .

"Roddy, hold on. Let me try something." He opens the camera function, points the GX-4000 at the white-tiled wall, and snaps a picture.

"How now!" Roddy exclaims in surprise.

A split second later, a rush of glistening mist pours out of the camera. Cooper has seen it before, but this time he's expecting it, and he knows exactly what to look for. He watches in amazement as the figure forms—arms, legs, face.

"Roddy?" he asks tensely. "Is that you?"

The translucent presence seems to be saying something, but no sound comes out. It hovers in the bathroom stall, the mouth moving urgently, straining to communicate. Then the shimmering figure is sucked back into the phone as if by a vacuum cleaner. A few remaining particles hang in midair, winking out like the sparks from a skyrocket.

Cooper taps the screen frantically. "Roddy, are you there?"

"O Coopervega, that was glorious!" Roddy breathes. "I was in the light, ever so briefly."

"I saw you! You came out of the phone when I snapped a picture!"

"'Twas beautiful," Roddy says in a hushed tone. "Thy world is a wondrous place, shiny white and adorned with divine sculptures."

"Uh, Roddy, I hate to burst your bubble, but I think you're talking about a toilet. You know, like—a chamber pot."

"Verily?" If a ghost can blush, Roddy does. "Thou must show me more—thy castles, theaters, cathedrals."

"We don't have that in middle school," Cooper informs him. "But there's a Gatorade machine in the cafeteria."

"I know not what that is, yet I long to behold it!"

A sharp rap at the stall door reverberates through the bathroom. "Cooper, is that you?" It's Mr. Marchese.

Roddy drops his voice. "Is that the watch?"

Cooper puts a finger to his lips and whispers, "My teacher." Out loud, he replies, "Coming, Mr. Marchese!"

"Is someone in there with you? What's going on?"

"No, I'm alone." Cooper pops the lock and steps out. Too late, he realizes his mistake. The GX-4000 is still in his hand. Roddy's image is gone, replaced by the usual home screen.

The teacher frowns. "So I *did* hear you talking to someone. You know the rules: No cell phone use in the building during school hours. If it happens again, I'll have to confiscate it."

"Knave," comes a voice—definitely not Cooper's.

He and his teacher stare at each other for an uncomfortable moment.

"Did you say something?" Mr. Marchese asks in an odd tone.

"Uh–uh, not me."

As he walks back to class beside his teacher, Cooper can't shake the feeling that he's carrying a time bomb in his pocket.

No, worse. A ghost.

What is he supposed to do now?

CHAPTER SIX
THE INSULT APP

"Good morning, Coop. Put your phone away and grab some cereal. You'll have to eat quickly if you're going to get to school on time."

"Okay, Mom." Cooper pours himself a bowl of Frosted Mini-Wheats and milk using his free hand. His other is clamped firmly on the GX-4000.

"You'll be a lot more efficient without the phone," Mrs. Vega tells him.

Veronica rolls her eyes. "Get a clue, Mom. He's listening to music. Can't you see he's wearing one of his wireless ear-buds? He probably can't even hear us."

"I can hear you," Cooper defends himself. "And I'm *not* listening to music."

"Why the headphones, then?" his sister challenges him.

"I don't want to forget them," he explains reasonably. "So I can listen to music on the way to school."

Mrs. Vega smiles. "Well, I'm glad to hear you're getting the hang of your new phone. Thank goodness for that."

"Oh, I'm definitely getting the hang of it," Cooper assures her.

"No kidding." Veronica is sarcastic. "He was up blabbing on it half the night. Who knew that a friendless loser would have so many people to talk to?"

"Veronica, be nice," their mother says wearily.

"He's snowing you, and you're totally letting him get away with it," Veronica complains. "Of course he's got music on. You can hear the buzz coming from the earbud."

She's half-right. There is sound coming from the tiny earbud, but it isn't music. It's the clipped English accent of Roderick Northrop. As Cooper pretends to fiddle with his phone while he eats, he pans the camera lens all around the house, giving the ghost his first good look at the twenty-first century.

"Thy dwelling is magnificent!" he raves. "Verily, thou must be wealthy beyond even the queen!"

"Shhh!"

"Yet where are the servants? And if this be the kitchen, where is the hearth? How dost thou cook without fire?"

The idea of explaining to a guy from 1596 how a microwave oven works causes Cooper to choke on a Frosted Mini-Wheat.

Veronica laughs in his face. "Swallow much, or just read about it?" A car horn sounds outside. "Gotta go. Chad's here to pick me up. I'll be late today. Volleyball practice."

"Ask Chad if he minds swinging by the middle school to drop off Cooper," Mrs. Vega requests.

"It's okay, I'll walk," Cooper puts in hastily. He likes Chad about as much as he likes Brock, which is not very much at all. And anyway, if he walks, he might run into Jolie on the way.

"There's no time," his mother insists. "I don't want you to be late."

When Chad's fire-engine-red Mustang pulls away from the curb, Roddy exclaims, "Forsooth! 'Tis a miracle! Where are the horses for this carriage?"

"Shhh!" Cooper hisses.

Veronica glares at him in the backseat. "Can't you be normal for one three-minute car ride?"

Chad chimes in. "I asked my kid brother about you. He says he doesn't know who you are."

"Tell him I'm Whatshisface," Cooper supplies. "That'll ring a bell."

As they drive, Cooper holds up his phone, giving Roddy a panoramic view of Stratford. There are cars and other vehicles, houses, stores, neon signs, and traffic lights.

"Surely not even Heaven itself can be so rich and beautiful!" is the young ghost's opinion, gushed into the earbud.

Chad comes to a halt along the school driveway. "This is your stop."

Cooper gets out of the Mustang just as a school bus roars up behind them and begins disgorging students.

Roddy draws in a sharp breath. "The galleon *Golden Hind* must have looked thus!"

"Like a school bus?" Cooper asks dubiously.

"*School bus*," Roddy repeats, trying the words on for size. "'Tis a worthy name for such a grand vehicle of a color so pleasing to the eye!"

Everything about Stratford Middle School is impressive to Roddy. The three-story entranceway—"Only the palace itself could be more grand!" The sight of hundreds of kids swarming in all directions—"Surely there are not so many children in all London!"

Even the video sign out front thrills the ghost to his core. "And this the palace gate. By what sorcery do the messages change by themselves?"

"You'd better get used to it, Roddy," Cooper mumbles into the GX-4000. "Everything runs on electronics in 2018."

"'Book Fair Today!'" Roddy reads. "Did you see that, Coopervega? There's going to be a fair! Perchance, will there be jousting?"

"Not unless the PTA moms get all worked up," Cooper tells him. "It's a *book* fair. You know—kids buying books!"

The ghost is astonished. "Are these children all of royal blood that they have the means to own such costly goods?"

"What's so costly about books?"

"In my world, books are out of the reach of all but the wealthy. Paper is nearly the value of silver. In my apprenticeship with Mannering and Brown, our books took months to print and our clients were of the nobility."

"It's kind of different now," Cooper tries to explain. "Books are pretty cheap. Most kids have shelves of them at home."

"'Pep Rally, October the Fourteenth,'" Roddy continues his reading as the sign changes. "What is this pep and why must we rally to it?"

Cooper soon realizes that it's impossible to answer all of Roddy's eager questions. To be plucked out of 1596 and dropped into the modern world is far more than the mind can absorb. When Cooper gets a drink from the fountain, Roddy asks, "Whence springeth this refreshment?" When Cooper opens his locker—"Seal me not in this coffin! Though I be dead, I have no wish to be buried!" When the PA system comes on with the morning announcements—"Hush, Coopervega! I hear the voice of God! Mayhap He will explain why I have come to live inside thy phone!"

"It's not God; it's the principal," Cooper whispers. "I don't think God cares whether or not it's pizza day in the cafeteria. Listen, I have to go to class now, so I'm putting the phone in my pocket. You'll hear what's going on, but you won't be able to see anything. And this is important—I can't talk to you, or I'll get in trouble. If Mr. Marchese finds out I've got my phone on, he'll confiscate it, and then where will you be?"

"In the clutches of thine enemy," Roddy concludes.

"He's not exactly my enemy, but he isn't the friendliest guy in the world either," Cooper tells him. "And if anybody turns on the screen and sees you, we both have a lot of explaining to do."

Especially me, Cooper thinks to himself. He's still not certain why he didn't tell his parents about the ghost in his phone. He's definitely worried that everyone will think he's lost his mind. He half believes that it might be true—that he's hallucinating the whole thing. Or maybe Roddy is nothing more than a malicious virus set loose by some hacker, and Cooper alone is stupid enough to fall for it.

But Roddy doesn't *feel* like a virus or a program created to dupe people. Cooper has played a lot of games and apps, and he's never seen an online character as real as Roddy. His accent; his language from a bygone era; his anguish at what's happened to him; his wonderment with the modern world— it rings totally true. No one could fake all that. For sure, no phone app could.

Which means Roddy is a *person*. Okay, a dead person, but he's very much alive on the GX-4000. He gets happy, sad, scared, thrilled, and disappointed, just like people who are still alive. There's no way to know why he ended up on Cooper's phone out of all the phones in the world. Maybe it was totally random.

But mine is the phone he's on, which means I'm the only one who can help him. If I tell anybody about him, the GX-4000 might

wind up in a lab somewhere, being poked and prodded under a
microscope by scientists, and Roddy with it. I can't let that happen.
I have to keep his secret.

He takes his seat in Mr. Marchese's classroom and opens his math book as the other seventh graders shuffle in. He notices that Jolie's T-shirt—NIAGARA FALLS TUBING CLUB— has long sleeves. That means the cast on her wrist must be off. He waves to her, but before he can catch her attention, a big body swings into his line of vision, blocking her and most of the room. Brock slides into the empty desk beside her. Catching Cooper's half gesture, he growls, "What are you looking at, kid?"

"Nothing," Cooper mumbles, focusing on the teacher's desk.

Mr. Marchese begins the day by going over the previous night's homework. As he leads the class through the sheet of math problems, Cooper becomes aware of a strange noise coming from the earbud—a snort at the end of a long guttural sound, repeated over and over again. It hits him— *snoring*! And it can only be coming from one source.

I never knew ghosts could snore!

"Roddy!" he whispers, hoping his low voice will reach the built-in microphone on the earbud. "Roddy—wake up!"

A long yawn comes from the earpiece. "Egad," Roddy pronounces. "Mathematics lessons art just as dreary in thy century as mine own!"

"Shhh!"

"Check out Whatshisface," Brock announces. "He's got a slow leak."

A chuckle buzzes around the room.

"Who is this knave who speaketh of Coopervega with such a poison tongue?" Roddy wonders.

Cooper doesn't know whether to laugh or cry. You can block the ghost's ability to see, but it won't stop him from having opinions on just about everything.

"All right, Cooper," Mr. Marchese admonishes. "Keep it down. You too, Brock. This is a math class, not a public square."

Roddy turns suddenly melancholy. "A public square. 'Tis an unhappy memory. The death carts gathered in the public square to collect victims of the plague. I beheld so many carried away thus—neighbors, friends, mine own mother. Without doubt, this was my final journey as well."

In the hall during class change, Cooper takes his phone out of his pocket and waits for Roddy to appear on the screen. "Listen, I'm sorry about the death cart and all that, but you've got to keep your mouth shut while I'm in class or I'm going to get a detention."

"The churlish boy who torments thee must be taught a lesson in manners," Roddy argues.

"Let me worry about Brock," Cooper shoots back. "You worry about the shutting-up part. Because if you can't manage it, I'm going to have to leave my phone at home and you with it."

"Prithee, Coopervega. I shall be a veritable mouse."

But in health class, when Cooper is asked to name typical allergy symptoms, Roddy begins to rattle off the symptoms of bubonic plague.

"Sneezing," Cooper begins. "Runny nose. Congestion . . ."

Meanwhile, in his ear, Roddy is making his own list: "Burning fever. Bloody spittle. Rotting flesh . . ."

Desperately, Cooper tries to tune his ghost out, but it's no use. "Watery eyes. Rotting flesh. Sinus pain. Oozing eruptions in the neck, armpit, and groin. Death throes . . ."

Mrs. Vostrov stares at him. "Hold on, Cooper. It's only hay fever. Are you sure you read the chapter I assigned?"

By this time, the entire class is laughing uproariously.

"Everybody stay away from Whatshisface!" Brock hoots. "You don't want to catch oozing eruptions!"

Red-faced and humiliated, Cooper notices that Jolie is laughing along with everybody else. That's the part that really hurts. At that moment, if Roddy had a real body with a real neck, Cooper would be wringing it.

"I am desolate," Roddy apologizes on the way to the gym. "I accept thy rage with a heavy heart."

"If I understood that, I'd tell you to stuff it," Cooper retorts. "Now listen, you can't come to phys ed because the phone won't fit in my shorts. You're going in the gym locker. It's not a coffin, so don't get all bent out of shape over it."

"I am a spirit, and am without shape," Roddy tells him. "I understand not thy words."

"Perfect," Cooper exclaims. "You've got a forty-eight-minute gym period to think it over." He throws open the locker room door and strides inside.

"Take cover! It's the guy with the hay fever!" comes Brock's bawling voice.

More laughter rings out as Cooper disappears inside a blizzard of sweat socks.

The only thing worse than being the butt of a joke is being the butt of the same joke twice.

Roddy is outraged. "Thou must speak up for thy honor, Coopervega!"

"No, *thou* must do what you promised and *zip it*!"

Flushed as much with annoyance at Roddy as he is with embarrassment, he kicks off his shoes, steps out of his jeans, and pulls on his gym shorts. When he pops out the earbud, drawing it through his long hair, Brock exclaims, "Hey, Whatshisface has that new GX!"

Before Cooper can slam the locker shut, the soccer star reaches in and plucks the phone out of his pants pocket. Cooper reaches up to grab it from him, but the taller Brock holds it just beyond his grasp.

"What do you think he's got on his home screen?" Aiden pipes up. "Maybe some of those oozing eruptions."

"Give it back!" Cooper leaps for the GX-4000 but comes up a little short.

"One way to find out," Brock decides with a cruel laugh. He presses the button and Roddy's image appears. "Whoa— it's some dude!"

Cooper can only look on in horror.

"Unhand me, thou rump-fed plague sore!" Roddy's accent rings out in a scornful tone. "Thy rank smell offendeth my nostrils! I would spit on thee, wert thou clean enough!"

Dead silence falls in the locker room. Even Brock, who ordinarily has an answer for everything, is struck dumb.

Cooper seizes the opportunity to snatch the phone out of Brock's limp hand. "Don't you guys know the Sixteenth-Century Insult App? You've got to get it. Here—I'll use it on myself." He holds the GX-4000 up to his face, willing Roddy to understand. "Insult me."

"Why shouldst I behave thus, Coopervega?" comes the response. "Thou art a prince!"

"Wouldn't you know it?" Cooper complains. "The server must be down."

The door to the gym opens and Coach Havermeyer barks, "What's the holdup in there? These ropes aren't going to climb themselves!"

In the babble of voices as the boys file out of the locker room, Cooper distinctly hears someone ask, "Who's Cooper Vega?"

Cooper waits for the door to swing shut behind them before turning back to the screen. "Roddy—what did you say to him?"

Roddy looks pleased with himself. "I spake no more than the veritable truth that he is a yeasty fen-sucked canker blossom. Thee should speak thus thyself, Coopervega, as it is obvious to any fool or beast."

"Yeah, well, it was awesome. I've never seen that big idiot at a loss for words before."

Roddy nods wisely. "Thy century is an astonishing place, filled with miracles beyond my wildest imaginings. But thy schoolmates art a band of slack-jawed ninnyhammers fit only for the employ of a chimney sweep."

"Vega!" bawls Coach Havermeyer from the gym. "What are you doing in there, baking cookies? Get a move on!"

As Cooper shuts the GX-4000 in his locker and jogs out onto the hardwood, he reflects that for weeks he hasn't had a prayer of standing up to the seventh graders of Stratford. And along comes this boy who died four hundred years ago, who puts the dreaded Brock Bumgartner in his place with a few barely understandable words.

CHAPTER SEVEN
THE APPRENTICE

Roderick Barnabas Northrop was born on October 23, 1582, in Whitechapel, East London, the son of Alistair Northrop, a noted alchemist and inventor, and Mary Northrop, who took in washing to make ends meet so her husband would be free to pursue his experiments. Mary died of plague when her son was only seven. Brokenhearted, Alistair lost himself in his work and Roddy was left to fend for himself in a poor and sometimes dangerous district of London, outside the protection of the city walls.

"How come you weren't rich?" Cooper interrupts Roddy's account of his life. "I thought alchemists could turn other metals into gold."

"Father was a brilliant alchemist," Roddy says stoutly. "'Twas he who first discovered that gold is gold and lead is lead, and no boiling fire, nor druid incantation, nor secret potion changeth that bitter fact. Verily were his achievements so great that he will never be forgotten."

"I hate to tell you this," Cooper ventures, "but you might

be a little bit wrong about that. There's no Alistair Northrop on Wikipedia."

The ghost frowns. "Wiki—?"

"It's like everything everybody knows about anything— and probably a lot of stuff they're not too sure about."

Roddy looks crestfallen. "O cruel world, to erase the accomplishments of a great inventor merely because his inventions all failed!"

Cooper tries to be gentle. "Well, if his inventions never worked, then what did he really invent?"

Roddy digs in his heels. "Many of the greatest miracles in your world began in Father's laboratory. The magnificence of your school bus—Father envisioned a great carriage, powered not by horses but by a force invisible to the eye. He also imagined a magical window—one doth look through the glass and behold not what is on the other side, but another place entirely. Is that not your television?"

"Well, I wouldn't go *that* far—" Cooper begins.

"And this phone that is my prison," the ghost continues. "Is it not merely Father's magical window of a smaller size so that it may be carried in the hand?"

"Not *exactly*—"

"So if thy Wicked Pedia hath forgotten Alistair Northrop, 'tis because the soldiers and magistrates believed the bubbling cauldrons and many-colored flames coming from his laboratory hath created the plague. In their ignorance, they tried him as a warlock, leaving lesser men to complete his greatest projects!"

"A warlock," Cooper echoes. "That's bad, right?"

"Very bad." Roddy nods gravely. "So bad that I was barred from working with mine own father. I was indentured to Mannering and Brown as a printer's apprentice. While Father stood trial for his life, I could not speak up for him. Mine employers would not grant me leave to see him before the execution."

Shame turns Cooper's cheeks hot. His own complaints—the frequent moves, his stints as the new Whatshisface in town after town—are pretty small compared with what Roddy had to suffer. Losing both parents; a job he hated; and finally the plague, a terrible and painful end.

"I guess it stank to be a kid in your time," he offers lamely.

"Alas, if only the unpleasant smell was the worst of it," Roddy tells him. "Chores that last through the dawn; mountains of paper to daunt Hercules himself; the stain of ink on my hands, my blouse, even my very tongue. And should the slightest comma be out of place, cruel Mr. Mannering would beat me with the bone handle of his walking stick."

"Sounds like a pretty crummy life."

Roddy shakes his head. "I had not the bread for crumbs, only a thin soup Mrs. Mannering made from supper scraps. Those were dark days, Coopervega. The agony of hunger rivals even that of the plague. Many's the time I thought of running away to sea. Yet a sailor once told me there were weevils in the biscuits. A full belly is surely a fine thing, but not if that belly be full of weevils."

Roddy resumes his story. His apprenticeship in the print shop lasted through 1596. What choice did he have? He was a destitute orphan, the son of a disgraced warlock. If not for Mannering and Brown, he surely would have starved. His days began at dawn and stretched far into the night. It was backbreaking work, setting type, cutting the quarto-size sheets into individual pages, and binding them into book form. Mr. Mannering was a harsh employer, never sparing with his bone-handled walking stick—especially when he would stagger back into the shop after a meal that consisted mostly of wine.

"I'll throw thee out on the street, vile son of a sorcerer!" he would spit at Roddy. "Thou wouldst rot in the gutter if not for my kindness!"

Roddy knew kindness had nothing to do with it. Mannering needed his thin fingers, which were deft with the tiny type of the printing press. His small hands— and the fact that Alistair Northrop had taught his son the rare skills of reading and writing—made Roddy the perfect apprentice in those days.

While his employer was in the tavern, Roddy eagerly read through the shop's freshly bound books. In those days, the London theater scene was booming, so most of Mannering and Brown's publications were plays. Alistair was too wrapped up in his work to be a theater fan. But a few years before—while the lab was being rebuilt after a small explosion—he had taken his son to a performance of *Tamburlaine the Great*. It was the most memorable experience of Roddy's life. In the print shop, he never missed a chance to talk to the playwrights who came in to oversee the publication of their folios. That became Roddy's plan, his obsession, his path out of this dreary and miserable life: He would become a famous playwright.

"That's pretty cool," Cooper tells him now.

"Alas, 'twas not to be." Roddy sighs. "The chills came first, then the sweats. By the time Mr. Mannering brought the surgeon, the dreaded buboes had appeared—lumps the size of hen's eggs. I was to share the fate of my poor mother, long in the grave."

"I guess it was pretty awful," Cooper puts in.

The ghost is stingingly sarcastic. "Of the plague we speak, not of a mortified toe. Yea, verily, it was awful. My memory is of much suffering, then less, then none, and finally of thee. The passage of centuries I remember not."

"Or what you're doing in my phone," Cooper adds.

"This I have pondered greatly," Roddy says. "Why am I come to thy world and not allowed to rest as others of my time? I believe I am here to serve a high and noble purpose."

"What purpose?" Cooper asks breathlessly. This could be important! If he knows why the ghost is on his phone in the first place, maybe he can figure out what to do next.

"To clear my father's name and restore his stature as an inventor!" Roddy announces grandly.

"Oh, yeah." Cooper is aware of a letdown. "That."

"Dost thou not see?" the ghost demands. "A great task has been left undone. I would wager my very life on it—had I still a life to wager!"

"Well, maybe," Cooper concedes grudgingly. It sure sounds like Alistair Northrop was a terrible inventor and an even worse alchemist, with no reputation to save. But how can he say that to Roddy, who has suffered enough? "Just keep an open mind, okay? We don't want to get locked into only one theory."

All at once, Roddy's eyes widen in alarm. "O Coopervega, I am unwell! I tremble!"

Cooper is alarmed. "That can't happen, can it? Ghosts can't get sick! They're already dead!"

"It is the plague!" Roddy insists. "First the weakness; then the fever! I remember it only too well! O cruel fate that I should die of it twice!"

The screen flickers, and Cooper flinches, as if the phone really does carry bubonic plague. That's when he notices the power indicator in the top corner—2 percent.

"Roddy, you don't have plague; you have low battery!"

"O wicked world!" Roddy moans. "To come back from the plague only to succumb to the low battery!"

"Low battery isn't a disease. It's—" Forget it. There's no describing it to someone from a time before electricity. "Where did I put my charger?"

"I need no 'charger'!" The ghost flickers again, his face suffused with panic. "Fetch me leeches to bleed the low battery distemper from my body!"

Cooper races around his room, looking under papers and books, and opening drawers in search of the GX-4000's cable. A chime comes from the phone, as the low power warning blocks out Roddy's tormented face.

"I hear the tolling of the bells. Farewell, Coopervega! Thou art a good friend, though thou canst not save me . . ." The screen goes blank.

"Roddy!" Cooper yanks the cable out from under a wadded-up T-shirt and leaps onto his bed, where the darkened phone lies. He jams one end into the port and another into a wall plug. Too late. The logo appears as the GX-4000 begins to reboot.

Cooper is stricken with guilt. He was so wrapped up in Roddy's life story that he carelessly let the phone run out of juice. What if he can't find him again? What if Roddy's spirit travels to somebody else's phone? Worse, what if the ghost is lost forever?

"Sorry, Roddy," he mumbles aloud.

"No need for sorrow," comes a jubilant voice from the phone. The reboot finishes and the home screen reappears, to be replaced a moment later by the image of Roddy, grinning from ear to ear. "Thou art a brilliant physician, Coopervega. I am much restored by your ministering. And without leeches! Thou shouldst become a barber, so great are thy skills!"

Cooper smiles in spite of himself. On some level, he understands that being haunted is no cause for celebration. But Roddy is more than a ghost; he's turning out to be kind of a friend.

Friends aren't easy to come by when you move to a new town every time the wind blows.

CHAPTER EIGHT
THEY CALL HIM THE BARD

Jolie's mode of transportation to school the next day is by skateboard—and, of course, she's an expert. She's just a blur as she flashes by Cooper. Recognizing him, she vaults up onto a low railing, leaps into a one-eighty, hits the pavement in a spin, and glides to his side. Her T-shirt depicts a lifeguard grappling with a prehistoric monster, above the caption LOCH NESS BEACH PATROL.

"Hi, Cooper!"

Cooper awards her a round of applause.

"Zounds!" Roddy's exclamation through the earbud confirms he has noticed her from the GX-4000. "She doth move like the queen of faeries!"

Cooper drops his phone into his pocket, casting Roddy into the dark. "Nice skateboard," he tells Jolie.

A snort comes from the earbud. "In the presence of such beauty, thou respondeth thus? For shame, Coopervega."

"I had to sneak out the back door so my dad wouldn't see me," Jolie admits. "I mean, I wear a helmet. Get over your helicopter parenting—not that he'd ever be cool enough to let me go on a helicopter . . ."

"Speak these words to her," Roddy advises in a confidential tone. "Say: 'Neither helmet nor veil should be permitted to cover thy loveliness . . .'"

"I like your helmet," Cooper says. "It looks really . . . protective."

Roddy is incensed. "That is not what I told thee to say."

Brock flashes by on his bike. "Looking good, Jolie!"

"Wait up, Brock!" She sails off after him on her skateboard. "Let's go check the bulletin board at school! The cast list for *Romeo and Juliet* is going up today."

"Bye, Jolie!" Cooper calls. But she and Brock are already gone, leaving him standing alone.

Well, almost alone.

"Explain thyself!" Roddy demands through the earbud. "Why didst thou not speak my words to the beauteous Jolie?"

"Nobody talks that way anymore, Roddy. And nobody says *beauteous* either. If I said that, I'd sound like an idiot."

"'Tis better to appear a fool than to become one and let a fair maiden slip through thy fingers. Not since my beloved Ursula have I beheld her equal!"

Cooper takes the GX-4000 out of his pocket as he resumes the walk to school. "Who's Ursula?"

The ghost's face turns tragic. "Only the best, closest glimpse of heaven on this sad earth. The daughter of my employer, Rupert Mannering. Alas, the attentions of such an angel were beyond my miserable grasp."

Cooper can't resist being sarcastic. "Why didn't you just tell her 'Neither helmet nor veil . . .'?"

"Mock me not, Coopervega. Cruelty ill becometh thee."

"I just figured, you know, since it's so obvious to you what *I* should say—"

"The penniless son of a condemned sorcerer cannot pretend to the hand of the daughter of his employer," Roddy interrupts. "But *thine* advantages are beyond counting. Thine ovens cook without fire and thy chamber pots need never be emptied outdoors. All manner of entertainments appear on magical windows large and small throughout thy grand dwelling. When thou strollest in the streets, not a single dead body must thou step over. Thou art high in dignity, Coopervega, well worthy of Jolie's love."

It brings a smile to Cooper's lips, and he walks a little taller. He may be the town Whatshisface, but at least one person considers him "high in dignity."

One ghost, anyway.

"Thanks, Roddy. But you have to understand the way things are now. If I go up to Jolie and start talking about beauty and angels and love, she'll dial 911. Kids don't say stuff like that to each other."

Roddy looks bewildered. "And what manner of 'stuff' might young lovers say to one another?"

Cooper shrugs. "I don't know. You mention that you kind of like someone, or maybe that she's hot, or whatever."

"Hot?" The ghost is alarmed. "This is a sign of the plague. Say not so of fair Jolie!"

"She's fine," Cooper assures him. "It's just that nobody says all that mushy, flowery stuff anymore. We leave that to Shakespeare."

"Shakespeare?" Roddy is suddenly alert. "Thou speakest of *William* Shakespeare? Short of stature? Ridiculous mustache? What knowest thou of him?"

Cooper stops walking. "Wait. Are you telling me you met the *real* Shakespeare?"

"Many playwrights visited the shop of Mannering and Brown whilst their folios were being printed," the ghost explains. "Marlowe. Kyd. Jonson. Shakespeare styled himself a member of this group, though he had not the wit to become their equal."

"Brace yourself, Roddy. In 2018, people consider Shakespeare the greatest writer of all time."

"This must be a jest! Shakespeare was a mere actor who fancied himself a playwright."

Cooper shakes his head. "No jest. He's the real deal. They call him the Bard—like you don't even need his name to know it's him."

Roddy is in true pain. "Such a cruel fate that my brilliant father should be so forgotten whilst a clod like

William Shakespeare winneth such everlasting renown that his work is remembered centuries after the end of his colorless life!"

"It's true," Cooper tells him. "We're doing a Shakespeare play in seventh grade. I'll show you the script. Everybody talks just like you. Maybe you can tell me what it means."

He slips the GX-4000 into his pocket as he enters the school building. The foyer is packed with kids, milling around the bulletin board outside the main office. Excited chatter fills the air.

Just as Cooper reaches the back of the group, a delighted squeal goes up in the crowd.

"I did it!" Jolie cries joyfully. "I got Juliet!"

There are congratulations from the boys on the scene, and some—less enthusiastic—from the girls. With Jolie snagging the lead, they're left with the lesser roles.

"Congratulations, Jolie," Cooper calls. "Never any doubt."

"Thanks, Cooper!"

"Well said," Roddy approves via the earbud.

Cooper works his way through the crowd, inching toward the posted cast list. He's almost at the front when a large elbow muscles him out of line.

"Big star, coming through," Brock rumbles loudly. "Oh, hey, it's Whatshisface! Check it out!" He waves his phone at Cooper and presses a button. A cartoon face appears on the screen and barks, "You're a jerk! The biggest!"

"I got an insult app too," Brock sneers. "And mine's better—if you pay extra, you get curse words." His sausage-like finger ascends the posted list of names from the bottom, coming to rest at the very top. "Ha! I'm Romeo. Naturally!" He struts off, bellowing, "Hey, Jolie—guess what!"

"Buffoon," comes a disgusted voice through the earbud.

Cooper scans down the list, heart sinking as all the decent parts go to other seventh graders. Finally, there he is—the next-to-last name on the page: *Second Watchman— Cooper Vega.*

Unbelievable, he thinks bitterly. While Brock is working cheek to cheek with Jolie, playing the most romantic star-crossed lovers ever, Cooper gets a part that doesn't even have a name.

Whatshisface has been cast as Whatshisface.

CHAPTER NINE
THE GREATEST LOVE STORY EVER TOLD

Second Watchman has only one line. It comes in scene 3 of the very last act. In other words, the play is nearly over before Cooper even gets to step onstage and say, "Here's Romeo's man; we found him in the churchyard."

He has it memorized within ten seconds of reading it in the script. Now what's he supposed to do for six weeks of rehearsals?

The answer soon becomes clear. He's expected to twiddle his thumbs while waiting for the chance to deliver his line. This is to begin right after school on the very day that the cast list is posted.

"Dost thou believe *thou* art hard done by?" Roddy demands. "'Tis I who must listen to the moldy words of that half-wit Shakespeare whilst my father lies forgotten in the mists of time."

"I could always turn my phone off," Cooper offers. "Then you wouldn't have to listen to anything."

"Thou dost not dare!" the ghost exclaims. "I shall hear

with mine own ears the dross that droppeth from the quill of this Bard of thine."

"Yeah, well, thine own ears are going to have to wait. Mom's taking Veronica and me for flu shots this afternoon, so we'll miss the first hour of rehearsal."

"Flu?"

"It's a disease. Kind of like the plague, but without the oozing eruptions. The shot keeps you from getting sick. They stick a needle in your arm—"

"Speak not of needles!" Roddy protests. "In the print shop, I stitched folios until my poor fingers bled, while fair Ursula braided ribbons in her hair, indifferent to my suffering!"

Fair Ursula isn't what worries Cooper. Fair Jolie is on his mind. Mainly, the tender love scenes she and Brock have to perform together. In a play like *Romeo and Juliet*, if you take out the romantic stuff, you're basically left with "The End." Cooper has to worry: What if Jolie gets so into character pretending to love Brock that she starts liking him for real? She talks all the time about how a true actress has to live her role. And for her, acting is almost as important as BASE jumping and wrestling alligators.

Sure enough, when Cooper finally gets to rehearsal that afternoon, his arm still throbbing from the flu shot, Jolie and Brock are side by side. The entire cast sits on folding chairs arranged in a huge circle in the gym, reading from their scripts. Romeo and Juliet are saying good-bye to each other in act 2, and the two lead actors are practically cheek to cheek.

Only one empty chair beckons, and it's obviously for Second Watchman. Cooper has to cross half the gym to reach it, and as he does, his shoes squeak loudly, dissolving the entire rehearsal into giggles.

Jolie breaks out of character, looking annoyed.

"Don't sweat it," Brock soothes. "It's just Whatshisface."

Cooper slides into his seat, red-faced with humiliation.

"Nice of you to join us," Mr. Marchese says in exasperation. "All right, let's keep going. I believe Juliet was speaking."

Jolie peers deeply into Brock's eyes and says, "Good night, good night. Parting is such sweet sorrow . . ."

Watching this is pure torture for Cooper. But what happens next makes him forget his agony. As Jolie continues Juliet's speech, Roddy says it over the earbud right along with her: ". . . that I shall say good night till it be morrow."

Huh? How can Roddy know those words? He said he never read any of Shakespeare's writing. He had no idea the guy ever got famous!

Brock comes in next, tripping over Romeo's lines: "Sleep dwell upon thine eyes, peace in thy breast. Would I were sleep and peace, so sweet to rest."

To Cooper's astonishment, the ghost recites those too, word for word. It doesn't make sense. Shakespeare wasn't Shakespeare yet when he hung around Mannering and

Brown's print shop in the 1590s. He was a newbie breaking into the playwright business. Yet here's Roddy, rattling off chunks of *Romeo and Juliet* as if he has them memorized.

"Roddy!" Cooper hisses.

Roddy continues to reel off Romeo's speech. He's better than Brock, because the sixteenth-century language comes naturally to him. But Brock is reading it straight from the script in his lap. Where's the ghost getting it?

"Roddy, what are you doing?"

"Sorry, Brock, I have to stop you there." Mr. Marchese stands up and turns cold eyes on Cooper. "I don't know what it says on *your* script, Cooper, but in mine, the Second Watchman doesn't come in until act five."

"Uh, yeah," Cooper manages. "I had to get a flu shot, so I missed the beginning, and I guess I got confused."

The director motions him toward the door. "Relax. Catch your breath. Take as long as you need. But when you rejoin this circle, I expect you to behave as a full member of this cast."

"Right." Cooper flees the gym, trying to ignore the scattered laughter and jeers that follow him to the exit. Once in the hall, he whips the GX-4000 out of his pocket and watches as Roddy's image stabilizes. "What's going on, man? Our play—how do you know it?"

"Know it?" the ghost repeats. "Coopervega, I wrote it!"

Cooper just stares.

"This I have told thee. I looked upon the playwrights in the print shop and thought what wit hath they that I have not? I would write a play of equal quality to the likes of Marlow or Kyd. Only the plague could stop me. And stop me it did, when my final acts were not yet complete."

"Roddy—what are you saying?"

"The words of fair Jolie and the bumbling buffoon—they are *my* words."

"You're lying!" Cooper accuses. "*Romeo and Juliet* was written by William Shakespeare!"

"I know not this *Romeo and Juliet*," Roddy returns stoutly. "My play is *Barnabas and Ursula*. As thou knowest, Barnabas is my second Christian name and Ursula is the love beyond my reach. My story was of we two—star-crossed lovers, separated by circumstance. I wrote on scraps of paper in the print shop when at last my labors were finished. All whilst your Shakespeare slept, or sat on his worthless rump, chatting with Marlow and Kyd and others of his betters."

It's totally impossible! Cooper's mind screams. *Ridiculous! Everybody knows Shakespeare wrote* Romeo and Juliet.

And yet, at the same time, it's so easy to believe Roddy. The young apprentice, slaving away on his masterpiece while the more accomplished writers watched their plays coming off the printing press. And when poor Roddy died . . .

"Roddy—" Cooper's voice is hushed. "Where did you keep *Barnabas and Ursula* when you weren't working on it?"

"Alas, I could not allow Mr. Mannering to learn of my manuscript," the ghost replies. "I had to hide it under my mattress in the corner of the shop. Even scraps of paper were too costly for the likes of an apprentice. Why dost thou ask?"

"You don't think—" Cooper takes a breath. "I mean, what if Shakespeare saw you writing a play, and when you died, he searched your things, found *Barnabas and Ursula*, changed the names, and took it for his own?"

Roddy is round-eyed. "Would that the ruff around his thieving neck had strangled the life from his worthless body! Did that snake believe that ridiculous names like Romeo and Juliet would conceal his crime? What other of my creations did he unmake? The setting of fair Bournemouth, mayhap?"

"Fair Verona," Cooper supplies apologetically.

"That knave! Shakespeare stole my play!"

"You didn't write any others, did you?" Cooper asks anxiously. "You know—*Hamlet*? *The Tempest*? *A Midsummer Night's Dream*? Are you the real Bard, and Shakespeare just stole all your stuff?"

"He must have pilfered those plays from other writers. Perchance he even penned one or two on his own. A teaspoonful of talent he surely had, for he completed *Barnabas and Ursula* before claiming it as his own work."

"*Romeo and Juliet* is one of the most successful plays ever,"

Cooper raves. "I'll bet every minute of every day it's being read or performed somewhere. Dude—you're a rock star!"

The ghost is bitter. "If it be thy meaning that my achievement is recognized only by rocks, then I agree with thee. I am doomed to be overlooked and forgotten, along with my poor father. And I beseech thee, Coopervega—speak not that false title *Romeo and Juliet*. It is *Barnabas and Ursula*."

As Shakespeare might have said, "Forsooth!" Or maybe that was Roddy's word too, and Shakespeare never said anything at all.

Cooper can't be sure what's true anymore.

The cast gets as far as act 3 and breaks for the day. That's not good enough for Roddy, though. The ghost demands to know the ending. How did Shakespeare conclude the great romance Roddy never lived to finish?

"I'm not sure," Cooper tells him, "but I think it's kind of sad. The full title is *The Tragedy of Romeo and Juliet*."

"Tragedy?" Roddy is aghast. "How can this be? 'Tis a beautiful tale of young love!"

That night, the two go through the script together, Cooper holding the GX-4000 over each page so his companion can read along with him. As the direction of the story becomes clearer, the ghost's agitation grows. Forced to marry someone she doesn't love, Juliet comes up with the idea to fake her own death. But the letter explaining the plan to Romeo never reaches him. When he sees Juliet's lifeless body, he's so devastated that he kills himself by drinking poison. Just then, she wakes up, finds him dead, and stabs herself with his knife.

The end.

A mournful wailing comes from the GX-4000. "William Shakespeare, thou art a monster! Thou hast taken my poetry and turned it into a massacre! Were we two not dead, I should murder thee for this crime!"

"Shhh! Not so loud!" Cooper hisses. "If my dad hears you, we've both got a lot of explaining to do—especially me."

"I care not! Barnabas—an extension of mine own self—and my beloved Ursula, both lying dead because of a mere misunderstanding! Shakespeare, *thou art the worst writer the world hath ever known*!"

"Well, how were *you* going to end it?" Cooper asks.

"Not with *death*, of a certainty! Love! Joy! Harmony! The two warring families would resolve their grievances and come together to assure the happiness of their children."

"Pretty different," Cooper admits.

"Not merely different. *Better*. Fair Ursula could never love me, because I was beneath her. So I crafted a story to show the world that star-crossed love is a beautiful thing. Thou dost understand this well, Coopervega, through thy unfulfilled love of Jolie."

"Whoa!" Cooper is defensive. "*Love* is a pretty strong word. I mean, I *like* her, sure—who wouldn't? But nobody in seventh grade talks about falling in love. We're, like, twelve years old."

"Ursula had but thirteen years," Roddy informs him. "Even vile Shakespeare changed this not, though he made a dog's breakfast of most else. 'Tis true that Jolie is not of higher station than thee—"

"She kind of is," Cooper interrupts glumly. "She's one of the cool people."

Roddy seems confused. "Art thou not—*cool?*"

Cooper sighs. "There are cool people and there are whatshisfaces. I'm so nothing in that school that nobody can even remember my name."

The ghost is suddenly angry. "Now I must pity thee? Thou, who dwellest with two living parents in a city where there is no plague and the chamber pots empty themselves? O, I weep for thee, except I have no tears, as I am a spirit— something else thou art not!"

"Okay, I get the picture," Cooper says, embarrassed. "You're right. I have nothing to complain about."

On the small screen, Roddy's features harden into a look of determination beneath his strange cap. "Thou shalt become cool, Coopervega. Fair Jolie shall like thee back as thou likest her. Mine Ursula may be long dead, but we shall prove that star-crossed love is not impossible."

"No offense, Roddy," Cooper tells him, "but how's that supposed to happen? You're stuck in a phone, and besides, you're more than four hundred years out of date. You have no clue how the modern world works."

"This may be so," the ghost says smugly, "but thou forgettest one thing. I am the author of the greatest love story ever told! If anyone can help thee, 'tis I."

CHAPTER TEN
FOUR FULL MISSISSIPPIS

Starting on Monday, morning rehearsals are scheduled for eight o'clock sharp—an hour before school. Cooper catches the early bus rather than walking. No one appreciates this change more than Roddy. Of all modern advantages over the sixteenth century, the ghost considers the "primrose-hued carriage without the horses" the most spectacular—with the possible exceptions of TV and Chia Pets.

"Would that my poor father could experience these wonders," Roddy comments through the earbud as Cooper stands at the corner. "He never lived to see his experiments bear fruit. O! The carriage approacheth. Prepare thyself, Coopervega!"

As the big vehicle roars up the street, Cooper aims the GX-4000's camera and snaps a picture. Roddy's translucent form whooshes out of the phone and makes for the bus in a shimmering swan dive. For an instant he's sitting, jaunty and transparent, on the hood, beaming back at Cooper, while the driver blinks in confusion. Then, in a swirl of mist,

Roddy is drawn back into the phone, chortling his glee via the earbud.

These brief "jumps" outside the phone have become a ritual between them. Cooper worries that people might notice Roddy's specter out in the world. But the whole thing is over so quickly that nobody recognizes the sparkling cloud as anything other than a wisp of mist or a splash of light.

Besides, it's Roddy's favorite thing. The ghost had such a crummy life, how can Cooper deny him this little bit of fun?

"Glorious!" Roddy sighs. "'Tis almost like being alive again, methinks."

"No problem," Cooper replies. Is it just his imagination or are these jumps getting longer every time? He could swear this one lasted four full Mississippis.

The door folds open and Cooper climbs aboard the bus. The first face he sees belongs to Aiden—obnoxious Brock's obnoxious sidekick. He's draped over one of the rear seats, surrounded by a few of his buddies from the soccer team.

"Hey, check out Whatshisface," he tells his friends.

Roddy's voice is full of urgency. "Thou must not allow thyself to be addressed thus! It prevents thee from becoming cool!"

"What am I supposed to do about it?" Cooper whispers behind his hand.

"Speak these words!" Roddy orders. "'Whatshisface thou

might name me, but had my rat hound *thy* face, I should shave its hindquarters and train it to present itself rearward.'"

"I can't tell them that!" Cooper hisses.

"Say it!"

Cooper turns to face the soccer players, struggling to translate Roddy's flowery words into twenty-first-century English.

"What are you looking at?" Aiden challenges.

"I may be Whatshisface," Cooper shoots back, "but if my dog had *your* face, I'd shave its butt and teach it to walk backward!"

There's a shocked silence, and then Aiden's soccer friends burst into laughter. Aiden sits openmouthed a moment longer before joining in. He reaches his fist into the aisle, and for an instant, Cooper thinks he's about to get punched. It takes a few seconds for him to realize that he's being invited to fist-bump.

"Good one, kid," Aiden says approvingly as they knuckle-tap.

"Roddy, it worked!" Cooper mumbles once he's sure the bus's engine noise covers his voice.

The ghost issues a satisfied "Mmmm."

Brock gets on at the next stop. "Hey, everybody, it's Romeo!" he bellows. "Wherefore art me?" As he lumbers to the back to join the team, he makes a point of elbowing Cooper in the side. "Morning, loser."

Cooper listens for the next instructions from his ghostly friend, but the earbud is silent.

That morning, Cooper finally gets the chance to speak his one line. He blows it. Instead of "Here's Romeo's man; we found him in the churchyard," he says, "Here's the church man; we found him in Romeo's yard."

It gets screams from the rest of the cast. His face bright red, Cooper wonders if he'll ever live this down.

"Sorry," he mumbles.

"I could train my budgie to say it!" Brock crows. "And he'd get it right!"

"Speak thus!" Roddy orders. "'My mind worketh not whilst low hangeth the sun in the eastern sky.'"

"I guess I'm not a morning person" is Cooper's translation.

It gets a smattering of applause and a lot of sympathetic nods from the rest of the seventh grade.

Roddy always seems to know exactly what to say. How can a kid who died more than four centuries ago understand more about surviving middle school than a real middle schooler?

As the day goes on, Cooper keeps the earbud in and his mind open to any advice his ghostly friend might have to offer him. Things go smoothly until science class, when, by sheer luck, his lab partner of the day turns out to be Jolie.

Roddy is enthused. "Fortune hath smiled upon thee, Coopervega. Thou must say this to her: 'Thy beauty shineth as the brightest star, lighting up the night.'"

"The book says we need a Bunsen burner," Cooper tells her.

"All well and good," Roddy says impatiently. "Now speak of her beauty!"

"Cut it out!" Cooper murmurs into his hand. "No—not you, Jolie. I—was clearing my throat."

She's gazing at him, perplexed—a look that suits her well. She pulls her lab coat tighter around her CARLSBAD SPELUNK- ING CLUB T-shirt. "Okay, what chemicals do we need?"

Roddy continues to nag as the two select various powders and liquids from the shelves according to the experiment instructions. His tone changes as Jolie lists the various compounds they've collected.

"Methinks I know this, Coopervega! This experimentation was first performed by mine own father! Thou shalt ennoble thyself greatly in the eyes of thy lady love!"

"She's not my lady love!" Cooper snarls when Jolie is away at the teacher's desk to get their experiment plan initialed. "And—what do you mean, ennoble myself?"

"This enterprise brought great acclaim upon my father!" the ghost insists.

"No offense, but it also got him arrested as a warlock," Cooper reminds him.

Roddy dismisses this. "Thou speakest of a different

matter. Dost thou not want fair Jolie to think thee more clever than the buffoon?"

"Well, yeah . . ."

"Then do exactly as I instruct thee: Increase threefold the amount of brimstone."

"Brimstone?" Cooper hisses. "This is a middle school. We don't have brimstone!"

"It is also called sulfur. My father described it as prince among all elements."

Cooper is a little reluctant, but he can't deny that the ghost has been a big help so far. There's already speculation in the seventh grade that Jolie is bound to fall for Brock just because of the roles they're playing. Cooper's sure not going to steal any of her attention as Second Watchman. How can he pass up the chance to make a big impression here?

He takes the measuring spoon, adds two large scoops to their mixture, and stirs quickly so the yellow sulfur is mixed in with the other chemicals.

Jolie returns with the signed experiment book. "I hope we got all the measurements right."

"Trust me," he assures her.

"Okay," Mrs. Anatoly announces. "All the groups are good to go. Fire up the Bunsen burners."

Cooper snares the beaker with the tongs and holds it over the flame.

"How come ours is bubbling so much more than everybody else's?" Jolie wonders.

Cooper is about to reply when there's a percussive *foom!* A flash momentarily blinds everyone in the lab. When Cooper blinks the dots out of his vision, he sees a plume of yellow-and-black smoke pouring out of the beaker, filling the room from the ceiling downward.

"Hey!" Brock points. "Check out Whatshisface!"

That's when the settling fog reaches everybody's nostrils. The stench of rotten eggs is overpowering. Cooper gags and drops the tongs. The beaker shatters on the floor.

Athletic Jolie leads the stampede for the door. The odor follows them out into the hall.

"Is it not glorious?" Roddy demands in Cooper's ear.

In answer, Cooper edges his phone out of his pocket, giving the ghost a firsthand view of the students, doubled over and gasping, as smoke pours out of the lab.

"Mayhap not."

Mrs. Anatoly shuts the door, hoping to trap most of the smell inside. "It looks like someone went a little heavy on the sulfur."

"Whatshisface made a stink bomb!" Brock crows.

The first thing Cooper sees through his streaming eyes is Jolie glaring at him.

CHAPTER ELEVEN
GO BIG OR GO HOME

If there's anything stranger than the voice of a ghost in your ear, it's having that ghost droning on and on apologies at you.

"O Coopervega, I do not blame thee shouldst thou hate me."

"I don't hate you." Cooper sighs. "I hate myself because I was stupid enough to listen to you."

"'Tis possible I was mistook," the ghost admits. "Perchance my father said *less* brimstone, not more."

"What was your first clue?" Cooper snarls. "The fact that the whole school is going to reek like rotten eggs for the next month, and everybody's blaming me?"

"Mayhap that is a good thing," Roddy suggests. "No longer shalt thou be called Whatshisface. Now thou shalt be known as He Who Hath Stunk Out the School."

"You're hilarious, Roddy. I can't get haunted by a normal ghost. Mine has to be a sixteenth-century comedian."

"I seek only to cheer thee," Roddy tells him.

"Yeah, well, cheer somebody else next time," Cooper snaps. "And stop apologizing too. I have to go to math class, and I can't concentrate with you in my head, whining about how you're not worthy."

The ghost apologizes all through math and social studies too. At after-school rehearsal, Roddy rattles off excuses about the difficulty of recalling exactly how much brimstone went into an experiment that happened more than four hundred years in the past.

They're working on act 1, scene 5, where Romeo and Juliet share their first kiss, so Jolie and Brock spend the entire hour with their faces half an inch apart. To Cooper's relief, they never actually *do* kiss, but Jolie is 100 percent in character. Either that, or she really is developing a crush on Brock.

For Cooper, that would be unthinkable.

As for Brock, he performs the entire scene with a cake-eating grin on his face, and is constantly looking around to make sure the entire seventh grade is watching. He bursts out with "Wherefore art me?" or "It is the east and Juliet is a babe!" whenever he senses not enough people are paying attention.

"I cannot live with this" is Roddy's comment.

"Good thing you died in 1596," Cooper murmurs back.

After rehearsal, Cooper comes upon Jolie taking off her sneakers and lacing on Rollerblades for the trip home. His phone is out, so Roddy spots her too.

"Coopervega! This is thy opportunity to plead for her forgiveness!"

Cooper is annoyed. "Because it worked so well for your dad?"

"I implore thee! Go to her and express thy remorse with a pure heart before she becomes the consort of that buffoon."

Cooper has had more than enough of apologies for one day, but the "consort of that buffoon" comment really hits home. He calls to Jolie, "Sorry about before. Science class? The Big Bang?"

Jolie cocks an eyebrow. "What's in a name? That which we call a stink bomb by any other name would smell like what Cooper and I set off in the lab."

It's a riff on one of Juliet's lines: *That which we call a rose by any other name would smell as sweet.* A good sign, he decides. If she's making jokes about it, she probably isn't so mad anymore.

"I guess I went a little heavy on the brimstone," he admits. "I mean sulfur."

In his ear, the ghost is frantic. "Thou art not sorry enough! Throw thyself at her feet ere the wheels on her slippers carry her away forever! Confess that thy love is so great that thou hast lost all reason, and thine only thought was to impress her with thy mastery of science!"

Jolie stands up on her Rollerblades. "Anyway, see you tomorrow—"

"Wait!" Cooper blurts. "I'm sorry!"

"You said that. No big deal—"

"I mean *totally* sorry. I was trying to impress you with how great I was at science. Only I wasn't as great at science as I thought I was. I feel bad that you had to suffer for my mistake."

She meets his eyes with an earnest gaze. "Wow, that's really honest."

"Bravo, Coopervega!" Roddy cheers in Cooper's ear.

"The kids in this town"—Jolie goes on—"they're nice and all that, and I have a lot of friends. But I can't shake the feeling that nobody says what they mean. That's what I like about the play. Romeo and Juliet don't care about what other people think. They're just honest with each other."

"Tell her that she hath placed her delicate finger upon the veritable truth," Roddy urges.

"I agree," says Cooper.

"I know people around here think I'm weird because I rock climb and bungee and parkour," she admits. "But that's being honest too—honest with myself. I love the thrill I get from extreme sports, the excitement. And the fact that there's danger—I get kind of a rush out of that too."

"Excellent," Roddy chimes in. "Now thou must say that verily thou lovest these things as much as she."

Cooper hesitates. This whole conversation started with her admiring his honesty. Why would he follow that up by lying to her? Of course he doesn't *lovest* these things as much as she. He *hatest* these things—and all things where a guy could *breakest* his neck.

"Say it!" Roddy orders. "Say that thou shalt be by her side in these amusements! Or as surely as night follows day, the buffoon shall be there in thy place."

Beginning to sweat, Cooper forces out the words "Me too!"

She seems surprised. "Really? I had you pegged as kind of the cautious type."

"Not me," Cooper assures her. "*Go big or go home*—that's my motto."

"Great," she exclaims. "What are you doing on Saturday?"

"Thou shalt follow her about as an adoring mongrel, worshipping her beauty and hungry for her every glance," Roddy prods.

"I think I'm free that day," Cooper translates.

"My family is going to Adventureland, but my brother's too little for any of the good rides. I have to go on all the roller coasters by myself."

"No longer shalt thou suffer so!" the ghost proclaims.

Cooper gulps. "I'll go with you."

"Awesome! See you Saturday!" And she zooms off, taking long, confident strides on her Rollerblades.

"Most excellent, Coopervega!" Roddy declares, immensely pleased. "Pray, what is a roller coaster?"

Cooper rolls his eyes. Leave it to Roddy to sign him up for something when the stupid ghost doesn't even know what it is. "It's a kind of carriage—"

"Like a school bus?" Roddy asks hopefully.

"Smaller and open. And it takes you up and down these giant hills, faster and faster until you don't know where your stomach is anymore."

The ghost is amazed. "And thou *enjoyest* this?"

"I wouldn't know," Cooper snaps, "because I've spent the last twelve years *avoiding* roller coasters. Thanks a lot!"

"To thine own self be true, Coopervega," Roddy chides. "Wouldst thou have told her no? Methinks not."

Cooper has to admit he's right. This is practically like being asked out by Jolie Solomon. A roller coaster ride is a small price to pay to spend a whole Saturday with her.

CHAPTER TWELVE
THE LOOSE NUKE

Adventureland is Stratford's own amusement park—not quite Six Flags level, but a world-class attraction on the edge of town, not far from the Wolfson estate.

The plan is to meet there around one o'clock. Cooper makes sure to arrive forty-five minutes early for some advance scouting. He gets a ride from Veronica and her boyfriend, Chad Bumgartner. Scanning the skyline of towering roller coaster tracks, Cooper can feel his early lunch climbing up his digestive tract.

"Well, have a good time," Veronica says dubiously.

"Stick to the merry-go-round, kid" is Chad's advice. "They don't call that big coaster the Loose Nuke for nothing."

Cooper isn't quite sure which of the three roller coasters is the Loose Nuke—the highest one with the near-vertical drop, or the loop-the-loop one where half the ride is upside down. Or maybe Chad means the one where you're standing up, strapped in like you've been chained to the wall of some medieval torture chamber.

Roddy's first view of Adventureland is more positive.

"Never hath these eyes beheld such revelry and joy. Surely not even the royal tournaments could match this splendor!"

"There isn't any jousting here either, so don't bother asking," Cooper tells him sourly. "The closest thing is where you throw a baseball at milk bottles to win a giant stuffed banana."

Cooper snaps a few pictures, not for the photos, but to allow Roddy a little exploration of their surroundings. In the bright sunshine, no one notices the shimmering ghostly form soaring above the crowd, checking out the various rides and games of chance.

Cooper counts—*one Mississippi* . . . *two Mississippi* . . . The jumps are definitely getting longer. Roddy's up to eight and nine Mississippis, giving him enough time to insert himself into a Ferris wheel seat or pass right through the giant hammer at the Test Your Strength booth. His spectral form briefly blinds the contestant, who misses the target and very nearly brings the mallet down on his own foot. By the time Roddy is sucked back into the GX-4000, the man is involved in a heated argument with the booth operator, demanding a free do-over because "the glare got in my eyes."

Cooper is curious. "Do you choose how long you stay outside the phone, or do you just get pulled back in again?"

"I know it as an urgent tugging at my body that I can resist not. How strange, as I have no body."

Cooper feels a pang of sympathy. It's easy to forget that

Roddy is a prisoner in the GX-4000, an exile from the distant past, and, most tragic of all, long dead.

Still, for a dead guy, Roddy has a lot of fun that day. He floats through gigantic tufts of cotton candy and vats of lemonade until he can almost remember what taste tastes like. He hitchhikes on bumper cars, which are practically as good as jousting. He hovers in the middle of the Tilt-A-Whirl, peering into the riders' faces and trying to experience their excitement. He objects to the thousands of stuffed animals on display as prizes, but once Cooper explains that they aren't made from the carcasses of real dogs, cats, and bears, he's okay with it. In fact, Roddy becomes obsessed with Ring Toss Tic-Tac-Toe, "a contest of great intricacy and skill." He refuses to stop nagging until Cooper has spent two-thirds of his money winning a gigantic plush unicorn, bright pink.

"There, I've won it for you. Are you happy now?" Cooper says in exasperation.

"It is a truly exquisite beast, worthy of a duke."

"At least a duke has someplace to put it," Cooper points out. "You live in a phone."

At that moment, the GX-4000 pings from an incoming text: *Meet me @ Loose Nuke — Jolie.*

The Loose Nuke. Why does it have to be that one? There are some nice, small roller coasters in Kiddieland. No such luck.

The sign in front of the Loose Nuke boasts that the main

drop is as high as a twenty-five-story apartment building. Jolie is waiting there, aquiver with excitement. Despite everything, Cooper is delighted to see her. This isn't school, where they both have no choice but to be there. It almost feels like a real date—just the two of them.

"Hey, check out Whatshisface and his enchanted unicorn!" an obnoxious voice booms over the carnival music. Brock appears out of the midway crowd, inhaling a hot dog in one titanic bite. "Pink is definitely your color, kid," he adds, mouth full.

"Hi, Brock!" Jolie greets him far too brightly.

"I didn't know you were going to be here," Cooper says, none too pleased.

"Veronica told me where to find you," Brock explains. "Knowing Jolie, I just went to the biggest, baddest roller coaster in the place, because she's a total beast."

Jolie glows.

Cooper winces. *How come this jerk can remember Veronica's name, but I'm still Whatshisface?*

The worst part is Jolie invites Brock to go with them on the ride. So not only does Cooper have to go on the deadliest roller coaster in three states, but he doesn't even get to sit next to Jolie. Brock steals the seat between the two of them, so Cooper is squashed between beefy Brock on one side and the stuffed unicorn on the other.

Cooper has spent a lot of time stressing over his first

roller coaster experience. It's a thousand times worse than he expected. The only good thing about it is that he's jammed into his seat so tightly that he can't possibly be flung out of the car to his death.

First the ride ratchets you up really slowly, groaning all the way, to a height unimaginable without a helicopter. Then you drop like a stone straight down. Cooper leans over to try to see Jolie, but Brock is in the way, howling at the top of his lungs. And through it all, Roddy is shouting urgently into the earbud, "What manner of suffering is this? Art thou being tortured?"

At the very last second, the car swoops out of free fall and climbs another hill for another drop. It goes on and on. It never gets better and Cooper never gets used to it.

Roddy had it right, he reflects. *We art being tortured. Yea, verily.*

Just when Cooper can't take it anymore, the car lurches to a stop, which is even more violent than the part that came before.

Jolie jumps off the ride, flushed with pleasure. "That was *extreme!*"

Cooper isn't sure he can move his rubbery legs until Brock pulls him out of the car, unicorn and all. The soccer star wobbles down the ramp to the nearest trash can, bends over it, and throws up his hot dog in a single heave. He wipes his mouth on his sleeve and roars, "Let's go again!"

All Cooper wants to do is find a quiet place to lie down until his stomach drops out of his throat, but there's no way he's going to leave Jolie with that giant doofus. This is *Cooper's* day, after all; Brock just horned in on it, thanks to Veronica's big mouth. So they go again. And again. They ride the Loose Nuke four times, the Cataclysm twice, and the Decapitator once. The Cataclysm is so violent that the unicorn goes spinning off out of the car on one of the loop-the-loops, and Cooper's phone almost follows it. At the last second, he's able to snatch the GX-4000 out of the air, but the unicorn is gone for good,

"Save me, Coopervega! What is this sorcery?" Roddy wails into the earbud.

At the end of the ride, the ghost's image on the screen looks a little pale.

Jolie is just suggesting that they go on the G-Force Free-Fall Parachute Drop when her parents text her to meet them at the gate because it's time to go home. Cooper has never been so grateful for anything in his life.

"It was so awesome of you to meet me here!" she exclaims, throwing her arms around Cooper and hugging him.

In that tiny, perfect instant, two hours of nonstop terror and gut-wrenching nausea disappear in a puff of smoke.

Then she spoils it by saying exactly the same thing to Brock, and embracing him too.

The two boys stand side by side, watching her run off to meet her family.

"Don't even think about it, kid," Brock tells him once she's out of earshot.

"What are you talking about?" Cooper demands.

"You know. Jolie."

"Hey!" Cooper's angry. "She *asked* me to come here today! *You're* the party crasher."

"Just remember who's Romeo and who's the loser with one line in act five."

They part—definitely not as friends.

When Cooper takes out his phone to text Veronica for a ride home, Roddy is there to greet him. "A triumphant day, Coopervega."

"Yeah, sure. You're not the one who's about to barf up every meal he ate going back to last February."

"Well worth the sacrifice," Roddy insists. "Would not Barnabas gladly exchange some small suffering to be near his beloved Ursula?"

"Barnabas died," Cooper reminds him. "Maybe not on a roller coaster, but it still counts."

"'Twas Romeo who died, thanks be to that thief Shakespeare," the ghost corrects him. "Barnabas was to win the love of his fair lady and live in bliss ever and anon."

"I don't think that's going to happen with me," Cooper complains. "You heard Brock. He's after Jolie, big-time. And he's got the inside track because she's Juliet, he's Romeo, and I'm Whatshisface."

Roddy looks out at him, his expression solemn. "Hear me. *Thou* shalt also learn the part of Romeo."

"What for?" Cooper asks dejectedly. "I'm Second Watchman—and I can't even get that right."

"Brock is a knotty-pated wits-to-let buffoon. He is unfit for a role such as Romeo. He will fail and thou shalt become his replacement. Thus will Jolie be drawn to thee. 'Tis foolproof."

Cooper stares at the ghost on the screen. Okay, Brock isn't a natural actor like Jolie, but he's doing a halfway decent job as Romeo. How can Roddy be so sure that he's going to drop out?

And there's an even bigger problem with the ghost's plan. "How am I supposed to learn all Romeo's lines? I won't get any rehearsal time because it's not my part."

"Thou dost forget, Coopervega. I wrote that play. No one knoweth Romeo better than I. I shall teach thee."

CHAPTER THIRTEEN
ALISTAIR'S MAGICAL WINDOW

"Cooper, what are you doing?"

Cooper shifts his position on the couch to peer up at his sister. "What does it look like I'm doing? I'm watching TV."

Veronica points to the GX-4000, which is propped against a sofa cushion, facing the television. "I'm glad you like your phone now, but isn't this kind of nuts? Do you take it to the movies too? Is it going to be your prom date?"

Flushing, Cooper takes the phone and jams it into his pocket. "I tossed it over there, and that's how it landed. Leave me alone."

"Zounds!" Roddy complains over the earbud. "I was watching that!"

Cooper knows there will be consequences if Roddy is prevented from watching *Wheel of Fortune*. The ghost has a major crush on "fair Vanna, the beautiful enchantress who maketh letters appear with a touch of her lovely hand."

Somehow, Roddy has turned into a dedicated TV addict and couch potato. Of all the wonders of the twenty-first century, television is his absolute favorite, surpassing even the school bus. He's convinced this is his father's "magical window." But not even the great Alistair Northrop could have dreamed that his vision would turn out to be so awesome.

Cooper sort of understands it. In Elizabethan England, pictures were drawings and paintings, period. The only moving entertainment happened on a theater stage. To Roddy, a cop show, with gunfights and car chases, is a real life-and-death struggle playing out before his eyes. "Forsooth! Be vigilant!" he'll scream at a hero, his voice reverberating painfully in Cooper's earbud. "He hath a pistol!"

"Cut it out, Roddy!" Cooper hisses back. "You'll bust my eardrum." And he'll explain, for the umpteenth time, that movies and TV shows aren't happening in real life.

"A brigand and an assassin hideth betwixt those walls!" Roddy persists.

"An *actor* hideth betwixt those walls. And his gun is probably made of plastic."

None of this makes much impression on Roddy. "What is this *plastic*?" He calls out warnings during action shows and cries during the sad parts of soap operas. During game shows, he marvels at the prizes, like trips to places he's never heard of, and home appliances that perform functions he can't begin to imagine. And he laughs uproariously at comedies, although he doesn't get very many of the jokes. If the laugh track is going, he assumes that a great many people are finding this funny, and that's enough for him.

The modern language he picks up from TV is even finding its way into his sixteenth-century speech in sentences like "Forsooth, the death cart is a major bummer" and "Chillax, Coopervega. Diss not the memory of my brilliant father."

Veronica has no idea of any of this. All she sees is her brother bonding with an electronic device. She sits down beside him on the couch. "Mom and Dad are worried about you. You're not making any friends here."

"The kids in this town are about as friendly as an open grave," he tells her. "And that starts with your new boyfriend's brother."

"The thing is," Veronica goes on, "we hear you talking to yourself."

"I don't talk to myself," Cooper says irritably. "I'm calling old friends. That's why they got us the phones in the first place, remember?"

"Save it, Coop. This is me you're talking to. You're not calling anybody. The bill just came in. You made, like, three calls the whole month."

Uh-oh. He and Roddy have been working on the role of Romeo, which often has them staying up late into the night. He was relying on the phone to be his excuse for all that talking. He never considered that the family cell phone bill would give him away.

"I'm practicing my part for *Romeo and Juliet*," he explains.

"Oh, please," she retorts. "Chad's brother says you have exactly one line."

"I want to do a good job, okay? Besides, I'm the understudy for Romeo, so I have to learn his part too. But," he adds quickly, "don't say anything to Chad, because Brock can't know about it. This is just in case he gets sick or drops out or something. Maybe Chad is smart, but it definitely doesn't run in the family."

"Fine. I'll pass that along to Mom and Dad. It'll make them feel better. They're afraid this latest move put you over the edge." Her eyes narrow. "You're telling me the truth, right?"

"Verily."

She freezes in the doorway. "What?"

He grins. "Sorry. Shakespeare on the brain. After a while you start talking like that."

A loud laugh escapes her. "You as Romeo! You think the world's ready for that?"

It doesn't look like Cooper is going to have a chance to be Romeo anytime soon. Brock is improving at his role every day. He's still not a great actor, but he's learning his lines, which are—let's face it—pretty hard. Cooper can relate. He spends his days struggling to follow Roddy's Elizabethan English. And Shakespeare is even more flowery and fancied up.

Brock is putting in the effort to make it happen mostly because he likes the attention. He's already the school's soccer star, but his status as an actor bumps that up to another level. He gets away with the obnoxious things he always does because now he does them Romeo-style—like pushing to the front of the cafeteria line, sneering, "Begone, vile Capulets!" or passing gas in the locker room because "farting is such sweet sorrow!"

But the main reason Brock is embracing his role is the girl he gets to romance onstage. As rehearsals progress from learning lines to actual staging, the relationship between Brock/Romeo and Jolie/Juliet continues to bloom. During the famous balcony scene, Jolie looks down at Brock with pure love in her eyes. Cooper used to believe that was her talent as an actress. Now he's not sure what to believe.

And if Cooper isn't too thrilled about it, Roddy is in full lament.

"Would that the plague had turned me to dust ere I wrote this accursed play!"

"I thought the plague doesn't turn you to dust," Cooper reminds him sourly. "You get oozing eruptions, remember?"

"I forgive thee thy harsh words, Coopervega, for I know thy heart be cleft in twain."

"I have no idea what that means," Cooper mutters, shoving the GX-4000 back in his pocket, "but there's nothing wrong with my heart or any other part of me."

It's a lie. Watching earth's favorite star-crossed lovers on the stage is giving him stomach cramps. When Jolie invited him to Adventureland, he really felt that things were starting to click between them. That may as well have been something that happened way back in Roddy's time. Since then, it's been all Brock and Jolie, Jolie and Brock.

After school, he comes upon the two of them, racing on Rollerblades down a steep hill and over a makeshift jump ramp they've fashioned from wooden boards and cinder blocks. They're laughing and whooping it up, their faces pink with enjoyment and exertion.

Spying him, Jolie waves. "Come join us!"

"No, thanks," he calls back.

"Art thou milk-livered?" Roddy demands. "Leave her not in the hands of that buffoon! Fetch thy wheeled boots and roll!"

"My 'wheeled boots' aren't even unpacked yet," Cooper tells him. "And you know why? Because I stink at roller-blading. I skate on my ankles."

"Alas," Roddy says mournfully. "Never did I believe my friend Coopervega would give up the contest so freely."

"There's no contest," Cooper tells him bitterly. "He won. I lost. That's the way she wants it."

"She invited thee!" the ghost argues. "I heard this with these very ears!"

"I'm going home, Roddy. And you're coming with me. Twenty minutes to Vanna."

"Thou shalt not distract me so easily," Roddy insists. "Mine Ursula loved me not, but there is still hope for thee. Thou hast not yet been voted off the island."

Cooper stops in his tracks. "Roddy, you watch too much magical window."

"Thou speakest without logic," the ghost accuses him. "Too much magical window—there is no such thing."

The next week, Mr. Marchese makes an announcement. "Congratulations, everybody. We're now officially halfway through rehearsals. You're all doing a terrific job. Give yourselves a pat on the back. As Shakespeare might have said, well met."

"If he could have distracted himself from stealing the writings of a poor dead apprentice," Roddy snorts into the earbud.

Cooper barely hears him. The gym rocks with applause. The seventh graders have been working hard. It's nice to know that their efforts have been paying off.

"In honor of making it this far," the director goes on, "we have a special treat. Every year, Mr. Wolfson throws the cast and crew a party to celebrate the midway point. Keeping with the romantic spirit of *Romeo and Juliet*, ours is going to be a dance."

Cooper isn't sure what reaction Mr. Marchese expected, but what he gets is a deafening chorus of whoops and moose calls, punctuated by a drumroll of foot stomping.

"All right, all right!" the director exclaims, banging a ruler against his clipboard. Gradually, the clamor dies down. "Let's try to be mature about this, people. Most of you are twelve or thirteen. Remember, Juliet herself is only thirteen in the play. If Shakespeare considered that old enough, the least we can do is not fall to pieces every time love or romance is mentioned."

Roddy's voice is bitter in Cooper's earbud. "Juliet hath thirteen years, for that was the age of my Ursula, and also mine own age. Vile Shakespeare had no hand in it, save the sticky fingers that stole my play."

Cooper swallows a laugh. For centuries, experts and professors have been agonizing over why Romeo and Juliet are so young. And the simple truth? Because that was the age of the guy who invented them.

"Lighten up," Mr. Marchese urges. "This is supposed to be *fun*. Think of it as the Capulets' ball, where Romeo and Juliet first meet. What an electric moment that is!"

All eyes turn to Jolie and Brock. Brock is beaming from ugly ear to ugly ear. Jolie's face is flushed, but even she seems pretty pleased about the whole thing.

This dance isn't going to be a celebration of the halfway point of rehearsals. It's going to be a coronation of Brock and Jolie as the king and queen of the seventh grade.

Why can't Dad get transferred again? Cooper thinks to himself. *This time to the moon.*

CHAPTER FOURTEEN
WHEREFORE ART THOU?

"O Romeo, Romeo. Wherefore art thou, Romeo?"

Jolie, dressed in Juliet's pale blue gown, peers out over the parapet of her balcony, delivering the famous line.

Cooper climbs the vines to reach her, the puffy fabric of Romeo's costume catching on the sharp branches. The way the stage is designed, he's actually ascending a rope ladder, hidden behind the greenery.

He gazes up in dismay—the more he climbs, the farther away she seems to be. The rope ladder is expanding before his eyes, and Jolie seems ever more distant.

"Wherefore art thou, Romeo?"

I'm coming! he wants to shout, but that's not in the script. He knows the lines, but how will he ever reach her to say them? What's going on here? Sets don't change in the middle of a performance! Rope ladders don't *grow*! He looks down. The wooden floor of the stage is fifty feet below him and falling fast. Oh, no!

"Wherefore art thou . . . ?"

Cooper climbs as fast as he can, until sweat stings his eyes and dampens Romeo's uncomfortably tight collar. But Jolie gets no closer.

Up the rope ladder races Brock, ascending at a super-human pace. The bigger boy muscles past Cooper like he isn't even there, mumbling, "Out of my way, Whatshisface."

"Hey—I can't hold on—Stop—"

Cooper loses his grip on the ropes and he's plummeting toward the stage, which is now too far away to see. The feeling of free fall swells in his stomach. He recognizes it from the Loose Nuke and the Cataclysm and—what was the name of that other coaster?

I'm going to die, he reflects, oddly detached from the moment. *This stupid play is actually going to kill me . . .*

Cooper sits bolt upright in bed, his heart hammering in his chest. What a night! He's barely sleeping at all, catching only small catnaps before uneasy dreams jolt him back to unpleasant awareness. Last time, he woke to the feeling that someone was standing over his bed, watching him. Creepy.

He checks his phone: 3:18 a.m. Nowhere near morning. "Roddy," he whispers. "You awake?" He knows it's a dumb question. The ghost is pretty much always awake. Only math class managed to lull him into a stupor.

Cooper frowns. There's no answer. Roddy's familiar face and odd clothing don't replace the GX-4000's home screen.

"Hey," Cooper says a little louder. He has to be careful not to wake up his parents or Veronica. They already think he's talking to himself. "Roddy." He counts to ten, then twenty. "Roddy? Are you there?"

Could Roddy be *gone*? Of course he could. When you think about it, there's no logical reason to have a ghost in your phone in the first place. A phone with no ghost makes a lot more sense than what Cooper had before.

But Roddy *was* there. It was no hallucination—not for weeks like that. What would make him suddenly disappear? Nothing changed.

Or maybe it did. What if something happened that had nothing to do with Cooper? The ghost always suspected his mission in 2018 was to make sure his father got credit for all his inventions back in the sixteenth century. Maybe at this very moment, a guy is writing a book about the great alchemist Alistair Northrop, and poor Roddy can finally rest in peace.

That means I'm free!

All at once, Cooper is aware of a heavy weight pressing down on his chest, constricting his airway and making it hard to breathe. He doesn't feel like he's been released; he feels like he's been abandoned.

"Roddy!" He taps the screen one more time, but nobody's there. And when the phone goes blank again, the darkness in Cooper's room is almost overpowering in its loneliness.

This is stupid! Cooper berates himself. *You've left enough friends behind to field a football team! What's so different about this?*

With that, a silvery shape flashes in through the window, circles the room twice, and is sucked into the GX-4000 with a vague slurping sound.

"Roddy?"

When the screen illuminates, the ghost is grinning out at him, Brock-style. "'Tis night, Coopervega. Thou shouldst be sleeping."

"Never mind what I shouldst be doing! How did you get out of the phone?"

"Thusly." The ghost closes his eyes, contorting his face in concentration. With a click, the camera flashes, and out comes Roddy in shimmering spectral form. He perches on the footboard, arms folded in front of him, beaming down at Cooper with a self-satisfied smirk.

Now Cooper understands his creepy feelings of being watched. They're 100 percent real.

"How long has this been going on?" he hisses.

Roddy offers a ghostly shrug, followed by a jaunty jig across the foot of the bed. He leaps off the comforter and is drawn back into the phone.

"Is it not joyous?" he raves. "O Coopervega, such wonders have I beheld in my travels beyond the walls of thy dwelling! A light in thine own yard possessed of such great intelligence that it shineth upon every passing squirrel, and yet not upon me. A red iron post on your avenue that is so revered by hounds that each one lifteth its leg in respectful salute. A manner of school bus that travels not on the ground but high in the air, with wings like a bird."

"Yeah, yeah, great stuff," Cooper says impatiently. "But did anybody see you? You kind of shine in the dark, you know."

"Alas, yes. Her body stiffened at the sight of me, and a shrill cry did she make. She chased me through many yards before I did elude her."

Cooper holds his head. "Do you think she'll call the cops?" The last thing they need is ghost sightings around the neighborhood.

Roddy's brow furrows on the screen. "I think not. After all, she is but a cat."

"Yeah, but if a cat can see you, a human can too," Cooper worries. "Some people get crazy about supernatural things. We could end up with a team of Ghostbuster wannabes combing the area. What happens if one of them notices whose phone you whoosh back into?"

"Worry not, Coopervega. I shall be the soul of caution."

Cooper is not comforted. This is the same guy who left his life's work lying around where a thief named Shakespeare could steal it.

CHAPTER FIFTEEN
HIPPING AND HOPPING

SOMERSET WOLFSON III
welcomes you to

THE CAPULETS' BALL

In honor of the cast and crew of

ROMEO AND JULIET

by William Shakespeare
KEEP UP THE GOOD WORK!!!

"Wow," Cooper says to Mr. Marchese, who is greeting the seventh graders at the door to the gym. "Is Mr. Wolfson here?"

It gets a big laugh from the students in line behind Cooper.

"Are you kidding?" Aiden crows. "The Wolf never slums it with us common people. He just picks up the tab."

"Aiden—" The director is disapproving. "We don't call

Mr. Wolfson by that nickname. And besides, you're wrong about that. He comes to our performance every year."

"Because that's *Shakespeare*," Aiden reasons. "He's president of the guy's fan club."

"They say he's got Shakespeare's sweaty underwear hidden away in that museum of his," pipes up another one of the soccer players.

Cooper snickers.

Mr. Marchese smiles tolerantly. "We'll find out soon enough. We'll be visiting the museum before the show. Although," he adds, "I've taken the tour many times. No underwear, sweaty or otherwise."

"The underwear must be in the secret collection," Aiden announces. "The one nobody's allowed to see."

"I'll bet he talks to it!"

"I'll bet he wears it on his head when he goes to sleep at night!"

The director makes a face. "That's just gross. Have fun, boys. Don't forget to take one of these." He holds out a carton full of colorful cardboard masks. "Remember—the Capulets' party was a masquerade ball. That's how Romeo and the Montagues were able to sneak in."

Once inside, Roddy asks Cooper to take out his phone "so mine eyes may behold the splendor of the ballroom."

"All right," Cooper whispers, "but you're in for a letdown."

"What manner of ball is this?" the ghost complains. "Where are the banners? And the tapestries? And the candelabra? 'Tis not a ballroom at all. 'Tis but the gymnasium, in half darkness, with a paltry assortment of colored streamers dangling from the basketball turrets!"

"School parties are always lame," Cooper tells him apologetically.

"I see no minstrels," Roddy goes on. "When beginneth the music? This rhythmic pounding doth bludgeon mine ears."

"That *is* the music," Cooper explains. "It's called hip-hop. It's pretty good—you're just not used to it."

"Ay! This cannot be so. The boys standeth by yonder wall whilst the maidens standeth opposite. Yet they danceth not."

"That's pretty standard too," Cooper informs him. "The last thing anyone wants to do at a school dance is dance."

"Thy world is magical, Coopervega. Yet the people in it tryeth my understanding."

The masks may have helped Romeo crash the Capulets' party, but for seventh graders who see one another every day, a small oval of cardboard isn't much of a disguise.

Cooper can't miss Brock's "Hey, check out Whatshisface!" and is happy to hear Jolie calling his name and waving from the other side of the gym.

Roddy sees her too. "Thou shalt say to her that her beauty doth put to shame the rose."

"You look nice!" he shouts back at her.

"Thou art hopeless," the ghost sighs through the earbud. "A lifeless stone knoweth more of love than thee. Thou must lead her into the dance."

"I'm not going to do that, Roddy. I'll look like an idiot."

Eventually, the teachers get so fed up with the boys and girls separated into two armed camps that they try to move things along by dancing themselves. If they expect this to inspire the students to follow their example, they're sorely disappointed. There's a lot of chuckling and even some finger-pointing. But the cast and crew of *Romeo and Juliet* keep to their opposite sides of the gym. They may be putting on a romantic play, but that's where the romance ends.

At last, the teachers resort to desperate measures. Mr. Marchese pulls Brock from his usual group of friends and marches him out of the gym. Mrs. Vostrov does the same with Jolie. A few minutes later, the two lead actors are back—in full costume. It does the trick. Two Stratford seventh graders are never going to ask each other to dance. But for Romeo and Juliet, it's the most natural thing in the world.

Of course, the play's star-crossed lovers never danced to rap, but that doesn't seem to matter. The entire cast and crew clusters around Jolie and Brock, clapping to the beat. Soon everyone is moving to the music, individually and in groups, swaying, stomping, and gyrating until it feels as if the very gym floor is vibrating under their feet.

The sight of Jolie, resplendent in Juliet's pale blue gown, dancing with Brock is enough to make Cooper's skull hurt. He points the GX-4000 in their direction so that Roddy can see them too. "Look at him," Cooper seethes. "He puts the Bum in Bumgartner! What a—a—*knave!*"

There's no response from the phone. The screen is dark. Cooper looks around and finally locates Roddy—a shimmering silhouette swirling above the dancers. Roddy has let himself out again—this time in front of every seventh grader in town!

Obviously, Cooper can't chew out the ghost *here*. Besides, the music is too loud for Roddy to have any chance of hearing him. So he holds the phone high above the crowd, hoping that Roddy will spot it and get the message: *Get back in or else!*

It doesn't catch Roddy's attention, but he's the only one to miss it. The dancers take out their phones, extend them over their heads, and start snapping pictures. Flashes burst in all directions. The deejay gets into the spirit and kills the lights. The effect is mesmerizing—strobe-lit bodies gyrating in what looks like staccato slow motion. And atop it all, like smoke above a battlefield, one sixteenth-century ghost, his puffy-sleeved arms and pantalooned legs grooving to the beat.

Cooper stands in agony, waiting for someone to point straight up and holler, "Hey, what's that?" No one does. The scene is wild, the camera flashes too blinding for anybody to notice the dimly glowing mass of ectoplasm circling overhead. Nor can they tell when Roddy's specter is ripped out of the air and sucked back into the GX-4000.

As the party rages on, Cooper glares in fury at the ghost, now on the screen again. "Are you crazy? Somebody could have seen you!"

"O Coopervega!" Roddy is actually panting. "Methinks this hipping and hopping is a most excellent entertainment! Perchance this be music in truth!"

The click disappears behind the pounding beat as Roddy streams out of the phone and rejoins the dancers. Cooper can only watch helplessly and hope that the deejay's lights cover up the swooping and swan diving that's taking place above them. There's no point in counting the Mississippis anymore. Seconds have turned into long minutes before Roddy is drawn back into the GX-4000, only to catch his breath and launch himself free again. No wonder the ghost had time to investigate airplanes and fire hydrants and be chased by a cat. He's learning to extend his jumps outside the phone.

As the Capulets' ball rocks on from song to song, a few other cast members slink off to the wardrobe room and reappear in full costume, much to the delight of Mr. Marchese and the teachers. But there's no question that the focal point of the party lies with Romeo and Juliet. They dance every song together and their eyes rarely leave each other—if you don't count the times Brock pans the gym with his puffed-up smirk, making sure that everybody knows he's got Jolie Solomon wrapped around his little finger. When he finds Cooper, the grin becomes almost Grinch-like, twisting his fat cheeks until it seems as if his face might break.

Cooper can't help thinking of the final lines of Romeo and Juliet:

> For never was a story of more woe
> Than this of Juliet and her Romeo.

Of course, Shakespeare was talking about the fact that they both died. But this feels pretty lousy too.

Eventually, the deejay takes a break and the teachers herd their cast members to a long buffet table for pizza and dessert. Roddy returns to the phone, exhilarated. "I am bereft. The hipping and hopping hath ended."

"Just while we eat," Cooper soothes. "You can get reft again when the deejay comes back."

The students, exhausted after a solid hour of nonstop dancing, fall on the pizza like starving sharks. Brock loads up a double-decker sandwich of four face-to-face slices, and Mrs. Vostrov rushes over with a paper towel to keep him from decorating Romeo's costume with tomato sauce.

"Why dost thou not dine, Coopervega?" the ghost asks. "Is the triangular flatbread not to thy liking?"

"It's called pizza, and I like it just fine. But something made me lose my appetite. See?" He angles the GX-4000 in the direction of Jolie and Brock. In spite of the entire grade milling around, it's as if they're having an intimate dinner for two.

"Thou shalt assert thyself," Roddy advises. "When the hipping and hopping resumeth, she must hip with thee. Also hop, as it is my observation that the two happen together."

"It's too late," Cooper laments.

"'Tis never too late—not even when the death cart cometh for thy sad remains. Behold—here I am!"

Brock reaches over to the deejay station, pulls off the microphone, and lets out an enormous belch. Magnified by the sound system, it makes the rafters ring. Then he bellows—his mouth still half full of pizza—*"I'm Romeo! Wherefore art me!"*

Cooper is seething. "I hate when he does that!"

The teachers exchange wary glances. They don't mind their cast and crew having a little fun, but when should they step in to keep things from getting out of hand?

In the nick of time, Jolie leans into the mike, and in a pleading tone, recites Juliet's lines: *"Deny thy father and refuse thy name. Or, if thou wilt not, be but sworn my love."*

"Yeah!" Brock roars, and repeats, *"Wherefore art me?"*

Tyler Macadoo, who plays Mercutio, chimes in with the famous "A plague on both your houses" speech.

Ruth Benitez-James—Juliet's nurse—delivers her line, filled with ominous warning: *"His name is Romeo, and a Montague. The only son of your great enemy."*

"Wherefore art me!" brays Brock when it seems like too much time has gone by without him putting his two cents in.

"Speak up!" Roddy hisses in Cooper's ear.

"No chance. I wouldn't touch that with a ten-foot pole!"

"Go forth and speak Romeo's lines so that fair Jolie may see that thou art better than the buffoon!"

And before he can think it through, Cooper is stepping forward to the microphone: *"Call me but love, and I'll be new baptized. Henceforth I never will be Romeo."*

As Cooper speaks, Jolie's attention shifts from Brock to him. At first, her expression is surprise. Then she steps toward him and delivers Juliet's response: *"What man art thou that this bescreened in night so stumblest on my counsel?"*

Brock tries to interpose another *"Wherefore art me?"* but all eyes are now on Cooper and Jolie. Even another tremendous burp doesn't recover the crowd's attention. As a last resort, Brock recites the speeches along with Cooper. It's his part, after all. He should know it best. But he falters, and Cooper continues on, letter-perfect. He and Jolie continue the scene—line by line, Romeo and Juliet—while Brock struggles to keep up.

At last, Mr. Marchese steps in, concerned about what

Brock's angry red face might lead to. "That's enough, everybody. Rehearsal is tomorrow. Tonight we party!"

He signals to the deejay. A few minutes later, the music is pounding, the dance floor is rocking, and Roddy is out there, flying high above their heads.

Cooper feels a hand on his arm and looks up to see Aiden regarding him in wonder. "Dude, how come you know that? You're one of the watchmen, like me."

Cooper shrugs. "I've only got one line. That's a lot of time sitting around listening to other people act. I guess I just kind of picked it up."

"Yeah, but you're a natural!" Aiden insists. "All those Shakespeare words. It's almost like you've got a little voice in your head telling you exactly how it's supposed to sound."

Cooper smiles. "You have no idea."

On the ride home in Captain Vega's car, Roddy can't stop raving about "the most glorious evening since last I drew breath in this world. And the crowning moment was thy performance. 'Tis certain that fair Jolie will commence falling in love with thee at any moment."

Cooper sighs. Roddy's great, but he has a lot to learn about twenty-first-century girls.

CHAPTER SIXTEEN
THE WOLFSON COLLECTION

Cooper stands in line, his hands jammed in his pockets, nervously waiting his turn to board one of the school buses. He can't believe none of the other seventh graders notice the ghost crawling on top of the lead bus, exploring every inch of the luggage rack. Luckily, it's a bright, sunny day, so it's easy to mistake the pale glow that is Roddy as an errant trick of the light.

At last, Cooper reaches the door and steps up into the vehicle. The next thing he knows, his feet are knocked out from under him, and he's flat on his back in the aisle by the empty driver's seat. His first thought is for the GX-4000. What if it breaks, and Roddy's got nowhere to go back to? What happens to the ghost then?

He reaches into his pocket, but before he can draw out the phone, Brock's big face appears about an inch from his. "Did you fall down, kid? Here, let me help you up."

He holds out his hand, but when Cooper takes it, Brock's

opposite elbow comes down against Cooper's sternum, pinning him to the dirty floor.

"Get off me!" Cooper complains.

"Hey, did you say something?" Brock counters. "Funny, the last time you talked, it came out all Shakespearey—like maybe you're trying to steal another guy's part."

"It's not my fault I know your lines better than you do," Cooper shoots back.

"I think it kind of is," Brock tells him, still pressing down. "You didn't learn them by accident. But this isn't about Romeo, is it? It's about Juliet. And like I said before, forget it."

As Cooper struggles to get Brock off him, a cloud of shimmering light swoops in through the open door and flashes into Brock's eyes. With a cry, he falls backward and Cooper scrambles up.

"What was that?" Brock demands. "What did you just do?"

The faint glow sweeps into Cooper's pocket and disappears.

"Nothing," Cooper says innocently.

"Don't give me that. You flashed me with a laser pointer or something!"

"How could I do that?" Cooper counters. "You were pinning me down."

"Hey, what's the holdup?" Mr. Marchese comes pushing

through the line. "We're supposed to be on a schedule, you know." He stops short at the sight of Cooper and Brock, obviously in confrontation. For sure, he's thinking about the Capulets' ball, and how the deejay's microphone became a battleground for dueling Romeos.

"I don't have to remind you two," he says sternly, "how important it is for us to be on our best behavior today. This is the one chance we get to see the largest exhibit of Shakespeare's material that exists in the world today. Remember, this is no ordinary museum, where you can buy a ticket and walk in off the street. This is a private collection. It's a privilege for our school to be allowed to view it—one that can be taken away if we don't show a proper respect for our surroundings."

Mumbling apologies, Cooper and Brock seat themselves on opposite sides of the aisle. The buses load quickly and start for the Wolfson estate. Cooper takes out his phone so Roddy can enjoy looking out the finger-marked and fly-specked window during the fifteen-minute ride.

At last, the buses pass through a set of magnificent wrought-iron gates, featuring an old English *W* painted in gleaming gold leaf. The roadway is lined with stately poplars, and snakes through immaculately groomed gardens. The mansion is impressive, with its lead-paned windows and stone facade. But it's obvious that Mr. Wolfson's pride and joy—the focal point of the property—is the museum.

"It's designed as an Elizabethan palace, in the form of an *E*," Mr. Marchese explains. "A long main building with large wings at each end, and a smaller central wing that serves as the entrance."

A sniffle comes through the earbud. "If I knew not that I was in thy world," says Roddy in a shaky voice, "I would wager my very life that this was Howard House, home of the Duke of Norfolk. Of course, ne'er was I permitted inside such a structure. Not I, the son of a warlock."

The buses unload and the teachers herd the seventh graders into the museum. Cooper spies Jolie up ahead, walking beside Brock. Fine. Romeo's got his Juliet. Jolie turns around, scanning the crowd behind her, and waves when she spots Cooper. He waves back, but by that time, her gaze has moved on, and he finds himself hailing Brock's unfriendly glare.

Although the museum is designed to look as if it was built hundreds of years ago, the interior is elegant and modern. Stepping inside, the first thing the students see is a twelve-foot-high bronze statue of William Shakespeare. There are oohs and aahs, and cell phones appear, snapping pictures. Cooper pulls out the GX-4000 to give Roddy a view, but is careful to keep his finger off the button.

Roddy recognizes the figure immediately. "And so we meet again, thou thief, thou snake in the grass, thou small-brained cleaner of chamber pots!"

A curator welcomes them, ushering them two by two into

a small theater for a video on the life and times of the Bard. For the students, who have spent all these weeks studying Shakespeare and learning *Romeo and Juliet*, it's actually pretty interesting. But Cooper hears barely a word of it. Roddy is ranting in the earbud, calling down curses, plagues, and a pox on "that jumped-up actor and false playwright who purloined my beautiful *Barnabas and Ursula* and turned it into a massacre!" When the ghost stops raving, Cooper assumes it's because he ran out of words, having used them all.

The video goes on to the life of Somerset Wolfson, and his obsession with everything Shakespeare. There are no longer handwritten manuscripts by Shakespeare himself in existence today. The only examples of the Bard's signature are a few old legal documents, now owned by Mr. Wolfson. Beyond that, the billionaire targeted the earliest published versions of Shakespeare's plays—the first, second, third, fourth, and fifth folios. In the centuries after Shakespeare's death, printers made changes in the text as they released new editions. Most of those changes were small, but they added up. That means that the first folio is the closest we'll ever get to what Shakespeare actually wrote. The Wolfson Collection, the piece concludes, houses more of those first folios than any other museum in the world—and more than all other museums combined.

When the lights come back on, Brock lets out one of his notorious "I'm Romeo! Wherefore art me?" announcements. He's shushed not just by the teachers but also a handful of students, including Jolie.

The tour begins, leading the students through stunning rooms with large glassed-in, climate-controlled cases. For a moment, even Roddy's complaints are silenced. "Mayhap these pages were printed in mine own shop!" he exclaims reverently. "Perchance they were read by fair Ursula herself! And lo—yonder press might have been touched by these very hands!" On the far side of the exhibit stands a sixteenth-century printing press in the process of inking a quadruple-size quarto page.

There's an entire display devoted to paper in Elizabethan times. No two pages are quite the same—different thicknesses, different cuts, different shades of white. With a click, Roddy leaves the GX-4000 and enters the case where the glass meets the plaster base. Cooper looks away, hoping that other eyes will follow his, and not notice the ghostly form swirling inside the paper exhibit.

"Don't do that!" Cooper hisses once Roddy is back in the phone again.

"Forgive me, Coopervega! To see such a wealth of paper hath pierced me to the heart. The very sight maketh my fingers itch to write another play. But, alas, to what purpose?

Evil Shakespeare would come back from the tomb to steal my work yet again!"

Despite Roddy's complaining, the ghost thoroughly enjoys the next gallery, which depicts Elizabethan daily life. There are examples of clothing that remind Cooper of the puffy shirt, vest, pantaloons, cap, and shoes that Roddy "wears" on the phone screen. The ghost points out several styles of dresses that "adorned the fair Ursula." At the sight of a mannequin of Queen Elizabeth I, Roddy propels himself out of the GX-4000 and tries to kneel at her feet, hovering just a few inches off the floor.

There are also suits of armor, weapons, cooking utensils, plates, cutlery, and furniture. "That dining table!" Roddy exclaims in a hushed tone. "'Tis a perfect match for the one we had in our kitchen."

"Maybe it's the same one," Cooper suggests in an undertone.

"Alas, no. Father's Brimstone Experiment Number Twelve caused it to explode most violently. I can attest to its superb quality, for it burned very slowly and gave off great heat."

"I guess Brimstone Experiment Number Twelve didn't go too well, huh?" Cooper commiserates.

"'Twas better than Brimstone Experiment Number Thirteen," Roddy laments. "That was when my father was charged as a warlock. 'Tis a travesty that Alistair Northrop has been forgotten whilst a charlatan like Shakespeare hath museums devoted to his false accomplishments."

Roddy's mood improves when the curator leads the group out the back door into Mr. Wolfson's scale model of Shakespeare's Globe Theatre. Cooper is amazed at its size and sophistication. With a capacity of nearly three thousand, the original Globe was larger than most Broadway theaters. There are three tiers of seating and a large ground-level open-air "pit" surrounding the stage for standees who could not afford a ticket in one of the covered galleries.

"'Twas my dream to see *Barnabas and Ursula* performed in such a place one day," says Roddy.

"Then you succeeded a thousand percent," Cooper assures him. "*Romeo and Juliet* is one of the most famous plays in history. It's been performed millions of times all over the world."

"Not *my* play, Coopervega. *His.*"

The class takes a few minutes to explore the theater, experimenting with some of their lines from the stage while their classmates report on the acoustics from the pit and the various tiers.

When Cooper reaches the stage, the glower he receives from Brock would easily melt lead. Mr. Marchese shoots him a pleading look. The last thing the director needs is a war between two Romeos.

"Here's Romeo's man." Cooper delivers Second Watchman's line. "We found him in the churchyard."

"This place is amazing," Jolie calls from the top balcony. "I can hear you perfectly."

"Big whoop," rumbles Brock. "Whatshisface remembers his gigantic speech."

"He remembers your gigantic speeches too," Aiden points out.

Brock glares at him. "I could remember all those too if I *studied*."

When the group reenters the building, the students feel the blast of air-conditioning immediately. It's much colder here than in the galleries they've visited before, and the curator explains why: This room contains the most precious part of the Wolfson Collection—the rare first folios. "Practically the voice of Shakespeare himself," the curator announces with reverence.

"Would that I could spit," Roddy seethes. Through the earbud comes a sound that can only be Roddy trying his hardest to spit. Cooper fights down the urge to giggle.

It's the biggest room they've been in so far—long, with cathedral ceilings flooded with filtered natural light. Dozens of display cases dot the room, each one containing a first folio under heavy bulletproof glass. The students are drawn to them like iron filings to magnets, peering down at the words that were printed there hundreds of years before. The boisterous buzz of over a hundred seventh graders diminishes to a murmur. Some of them read quietly. Most just stare. Shakespeare fan or no, everyone understands that they are looking at objects of incredible age and value.

"Coopervega." Roddy's voice is urgent in the earbud. "There is something here."

"Yeah," Cooper whispers. "The first folios." He holds up the GX-4000 to give the ghost a better look. The ancient book is open to *Hamlet*, and Cooper can make out the line: *To thine own self be true.* Roddy said that once. Maybe the ghost had more in common with Shakespeare than he likes to admit.

"Not this rubbish," Roddy insists. "I feel something of great strength summoning me, beckoning."

"One of the displays?" Cooper asks.

"I know not. Yet methinks I feel the attraction coming from beyond yonder door."

"Yonder?" Cooper queries. Then he sees it. An interior wall stretches the full length of the gallery. It's white and featureless, with one exception. There is an almost invisible door at the far end, frameless, with no knob and only a recessed keyhole.

"The secret collection!" Cooper exclaims.

"I understand this not."

"It's just a rumor," Cooper tells Roddy in a low voice. "But everyone says The Wolf has a whole stash of secret stuff that he can't display because he's not supposed to own it. Maybe what's calling you is something in there!"

And then a new voice—deep and resonant, but with a childlike enthusiasm—rings out through the galleria: "Welcome to the Wolfson Collection!"

Into their midst strides a stocky man of medium height, a shock of white hair brushed straight back from his high forehead. Although he's never met the newcomer, Cooper recognizes him immediately from TV and newspapers.

It's Somerset Wolfson, their billionaire host.

CHAPTER SEVENTEEN
PUBLIC ENEMY NUMBER ONE

At the urging of the teachers, all the students gather around Stratford's wealthiest citizen.

"I'm hearing great things about your progress in rehearsal, and I can't wait to be there in the front row on opening night of *Romeo and Juliet*," the billionaire tells them. "You know, when your little community offered me such a warm welcome, I thought of all the ways that I could give back. And the greatest gift I have is my love of the Bard of Avon, William Shakespeare, the most superlative playwright and poet this world has ever produced."

"This attraction is most mysterious," Roddy intones through the earbud. "Methinks I cannot resist it."

"Shhh!" Cooper hisses.

"Excuse me?" Mr. Wolfson's sharp gaze is suddenly riveted on Cooper. "You have a question?"

"Oh, sorry to interrupt—"

"Nonsense." Mr. Wolfson beams. "I'm anxious to hear

your take on what you've seen. First things first—what is your role in *Romeo and Juliet?*"

"I'm"—Cooper reddens—"Second Watchman."

An amused chuckle breezes through the student body.

The billionaire smiles tolerantly. "Every role, no matter how small, represents a vital part of Shakespeare's genius vision. Now, what is your question, young man?"

"Oh, I don't have a—" Cooper begins.

"The door!" Roddy exclaims via the earbud. "Ask about the door!"

"What's behind that door over there?" Cooper blurts.

Mr. Wolfson's smile disappears. "That's just a storage room."

"Storage for what?" Cooper persists.

"Really, young man." The billionaire is losing patience. "We're surrounded by such treasures as most people only dream of seeing, and all you can think of is where the mops and brooms are kept?"

"I must see for myself!" Roddy announces in the earbud. There is a click and the ghost's spectral form begins to rise out of the phone.

Cooper does the only thing he can think of to distract everyone's attention from Roddy's escape: He launches into a coughing fit that has him hugging one of the display cases and fogging the glass. Out of the corner of his eye, he spies the ghost sailing over heads and first folios down the long room to the mystery door. There, he reshapes himself into a long, thin ribbon and wafts in through the keyhole.

At last, Cooper straightens up and attempts to clean off the glass with his sleeve.

"Never mind that!" Mr. Wolfson snaps, irritated. "Does anyone have a *real* question? You've just taken a tour through the most complete collection in the world of the works of the one true Bard—"

"Are you sure he's as true as you think he is?" Cooper interrupts.

Mr. Marchese shoots him a warning look.

"You're speaking of the theory that some of Shakespeare's works were written by other playwrights of the time," the billionaire says stiffly. "It's all nonsense, of course. No serious scholar believes that."

"What about *Barnabas and Ursula*?" Cooper challenges.

Mr. Wolfson's shock is too genuine to be faked. His face turns brick red and his eyes bulge. He opens his mouth to speak, but no sound comes out.

All eyes turn to Cooper. No one can remember ever seeing the great Somerset Wolfson so completely at a loss.

"I don't get it," puts in Brock in a loud voice. "Who are Barnabas and Ursula?"

The billionaire finds his voice at last. "I believe this tour has come to an end," he says in a subdued tone that is a shadow of his enthusiastic welcome. "Your buses will be waiting in the main driveway." Without another word, he leaves them, wending his way among the display cases to an exit.

"I don't know what just happened," Brock announces with a laugh. "But it was definitely Whatshisface's fault."

"That's enough." Mr. Marchese's face is unnaturally pale. "We've never been asked to leave before. This is a disaster. Now form a line, and let's go."

"But—we're not ready to go," Cooper protests. He's in a panic. What about Roddy, who is still in the secret room? "We haven't looked at all these great first folios yet."

The director is angry. "I hope you're kidding, Cooper. You can't be the only one who missed the fact that we've been kicked out—and probably because of you. I don't know what you said back there, but it clearly upset Mr. Wolfson. Now move it along."

Hoping to stall for time, Cooper shuffles to the back of the line. He gets a lot of dirty looks from his fellow cast members. Everybody knows who Whatshisface is now. He's public enemy number one.

Only Brock has a smile for him. "Smooth move, Romeo. Wherefore art your brains?"

Jolie regards Cooper sadly. "What if Mr. Wolfson doesn't come to our show?"

She looks disappointed. The last thing Cooper wants is to disappoint her. In that moment, he feels more like an outsider than ever before. No local would ever risk insulting Mr. Wolfson in his own museum. It takes the new guy to do that.

Yet as upset as Cooper is, he's even more worried about Roddy. As the group from the middle school marches out of the gallery, he keeps an eye on the mysterious door, hoping against hope to see Roddy's spectral form heading for home in the GX-4000.

No luck.

Cooper pauses at the museum's front door. *Come on, Roddy! Where are you?*

"Hurry up, Cooper," Mr. Marchese prods. "Why are you dragging your feet?"

"I—I should probably go to the bathroom before the drive," Cooper stammers.

"We'll be at school in fifteen minutes. You can make it that long."

Yes, but can Roddy? What if the phone isn't there to receive him when he's done exploring the secret room? Sure, the ghost is able to cover some distance when he's out exploring, but in those cases Roddy always knew where home base was. The phone wasn't getting on a bus to travel halfway across town. What if Roddy can't find his way back? What if he can't travel that far? What happens to a ghost who has no place to go? Obviously, Roddy can't *die*—that happened a long time ago. But will he be doomed to wander forever?

Cooper shuffles across the driveway. All three buses are loaded now. The first two are pulling away. Mr. Marchese stands at the entrance to the third, twirling one arm in a gesture of impatience. As Cooper steps aboard, he considers going down with a twisted ankle. No, the director will never buy it. Neither will the other kids. He scans the bus for a friendly face and comes up empty.

The door closes behind him and the bus's engine roars to life.

Sorry, Roddy. I tried—

They head down the drive and are just about to pass through the gates when a shimmering cloud shoots out of one of the museum skylights and makes a beeline for the bus. Cooper spots it through the emergency door in the back— Roddy, in hot pursuit.

He leaps into the aisle and barks, "Stop!"

The driver glances at him in the rearview mirror. "Sit down, you."

Mr. Marchese has reached the end of his rope. "Take your seat!"

From the row behind, Brock reaches up, grabs Cooper by the back of the collar, and hauls him down to the bench.

Since all eyes are on Cooper, nobody sees the blob of faint shimmering light attach itself to the bus's emergency door. It hangs there for a brief second, then oozes inside through a tiny crack in the glass. A split second later, it slips into Cooper's pocket and disappears.

Weak with relief, Cooper slumps in his seat. Roddy is safe. That's all that matters.

Barely have Cooper's shoulders touched the backrest when the earbud bursts to life.

"'Tis there, Coopervega! I have seen it with these very eyes!"

"What?" Cooper whispers.

"Barnabas and Ursula," comes the supercharged reply. "The play that I never lived to finish. 'Tis there, verily—and in mine own hand."

CHAPTER EIGHTEEN
PROOF POSITIVE

For the rest of the day, Cooper's mind is awhirl. There are so many things he has to ask Roddy, but back at school, that's impossible. Mr. Marchese has been watching him like a hawk ever since his strange behavior at the Wolfson Collection. His fellow students are all over him too, curious about his altercation with Stratford's most famous resident. Being Whatshisface wasn't fun, but at least he could rely on having a little privacy. Now he's the nutjob who got the entire seventh grade kicked out of the museum, and everyone is interested in what makes him tick and why. Even in the seclusion of a bathroom stall, he's aware of his next-door neighbor, possibly listening in. The last thing he can risk is a long one-sided conversation with the ghost on his cell phone.

But the suspense is killing him. Roddy has so much to tell him. The secret collection is *real*! And it has the ghost's original manuscript in it!

To make matters worse, Roddy hasn't shut up since his arrival back on the bus. As Cooper tries to struggle through the rest of the day without getting anyone else mad at him, his head is being filled with endless details of the secret gallery behind the door—costumes and props from Shakespeare's career as an actor; furniture and clothing from his house in Stratford-upon-Avon; documents with his signature, including his certificate of marriage to one Anne Hathaway.

"And each of these objects doth bear a seal or marking proclaiming that it be property of a great museum or library," Roddy concludes. "Dost thou not see? These things are hidden behind a locked door because they are stolen, just as surely as *Barnabas and Ursula* was stolen from me by Shakespeare himself!"

"I get it," Cooper hisses. "I just can't talk right now."

"But, Coopervega, thou must listen to me!"

It gets so bad that Cooper removes the wireless earbud. He can feel it in his pockets, buzzing away as the ghost goes on and on. Insulted, Roddy lets himself out of the phone and circles Cooper's head, shaking a shimmering fist—a highly risky move in the middle of social studies class.

After school, in the privacy of his room, Cooper pops the earbud back in.

Roddy sounds a little insulted. "Forsooth. *Now* thou hast time for me." Elizabethan sarcasm.

"Sorry," Cooper apologizes. "It's just that this is a huge thing we have to talk out, and there's no way I could have done that in the middle of school—not after I got into that beef with The Wolf."

"Beef?" Roddy queries. "I wasn't aware that dinner was served."

"Never mind that. The point is the guy's a crook, with a secret gallery full of stolen artifacts that he can't show anybody or he'll get busted—you know, the watch will come after him."

"There is but one part I understand not," the ghost says, frowning in concentration on the screen. "The Wolf cannot exhibit the stolen items—this is as clear as the dawn. But why doth he conceal *Barnabas and Ursula*? Yea, it was stolen, verily. But by Shakespeare, not by him. And it is too late to arrest Shakespeare—though a more welcome addition to Tyburn Gallows I cannot imagine."

"Don't you get it?" Cooper explains. "If The Wolf displayed *Barnabas and Ursula*, that would show the whole world proof positive that Shakespeare ripped off *Romeo and Juliet*—the first three-quarters of it, anyway. Basically, he'd be admitting that he devoted his entire life and fortune to a big fake. He even made the people around here change the name of their town to Stratford in honor of you know who. And if the great William Shakespeare jacked one of his most famous plays, you've got to wonder what else he helped himself to. His reputation would be basically shot. Trust me, the last thing The Wolf wants is for anybody to find out about *Barnabas and Ursula*."

"Thou must shout it from the rooftops!" Roddy insists.

"You're not serious. You remember what it's like to be a kid? Did anybody listen to you in 1596? Well, it isn't any different today! What am I supposed to do? Call up the newspaper and say, 'You know that playwright everybody thinks is the greatest genius of all time? Well, he's a phony! And how do I know? My pet ghost told me.' Yeah—that'll work."

"Thou hast reason, Coopervega," Roddy concedes. "But the solution is simple. *I* shall accompany thee! No man can deny the existence of a ghost that he sees with his own eyes, even if that ghost doth appear only on a phone."

"It's too dangerous," Cooper tells him.

"Thou needst not worry that I might be killed. That galleon hath already set sail."

"It's not that," Cooper explains. "Most people don't believe in ghosts in my world. If I let anybody see you, every scientist in the world is going to come down on us. They'll take the phone apart circuit by circuit until there's nothing left but dust. And what happens to you? Where will you go? Will you have to wander forever, nothing but a cloud of sparkles? Will you just disappear?"

"Thou paintest a grim picture," Roddy laments. "Verily,

my time was cruel with the plague, harsh laws, and grinding poverty. But what improvements hath the centuries brought if there is no justice for my *Barnabas and Ursula*?"

"It stinks," Cooper agrees, "but there's nothing we can do about it. The performance is on Saturday. Tomorrow the evening rehearsals start. We aren't going to have time for anything but *Romeo and Juliet*. Sorry, Roddy."

"'Tis not thy fault, Coopervega," says Roddy.

But Cooper detects an expression on the ghost's face that he can't quite identify.

CHAPTER NINETEEN
THE KILLER CLOUD

With the performance just a few days away, the seventh grade kicks into high gear. It's tech week, where every rehearsal is a full dress rehearsal. The morning sessions are canceled—Mr. Marchese wants his cast and crew well rested. But afternoon run-through now stretches from the end of school until six p.m. And every night, after a quick dinner, the students rush back to work until almost ten.

Cast members with smaller roles, like Cooper and Aiden, are recruited to help the staging crew finalize the sets, attaching rollers for quick and silent scene changes. The spotlights are lovingly nudged into position overhead. The teachers walk around with dazed looks on their faces, as if they're hunted animals who haven't slept in weeks. Mr. Marchese is never seen without his script, which is such a mass of scribbles and Post-it Notes that it resembles the giant head of a monster about to eat him.

The halls ring with *forsooth*s and *methinks*es. It isn't a big change for Cooper, who hears such words regularly through his earbud. But for the students of Stratford Middle School, it means one thing: Zero hour is bearing down on them.

Another perk: Homework is suspended until after the performance. There wouldn't be enough time to do it anyway. The cast and crew are stretched to the limit. Night after night, Cooper falls asleep on the living room couch, leaving the GX-4000 propped on the pillows so Roddy can watch reruns of *The Big Bang Theory.*

Without the a.m. casting calls, mornings are a lot less stressful. No longer does Cooper have to scramble to catch the early bus. He can walk to school at a leisurely pace.

The only drawback is Brock and Jolie. With marathon rehearsals taking up practically every spare minute, Romeo and Juliet have become closer than ever. It's especially painful to Cooper. At the Capulets' ball, it really seemed as if Jolie was gravitating away from Brock and in Cooper's direction. Not anymore. The disaster at the Wolfson museum put an end to that. Cooper made an idiot out of himself in front of the entire seventh grade, and ticked off Stratford's resident VIP in the process. According to the latest scuttlebutt, the billionaire is still planning to attend *Romeo and Juliet.* But everybody knows for sure that's in spite of Cooper, not because of him.

How could it be worse? There's probably some way, but Cooper sure can't think of one. Brock and Jolie have been inseparable all through tech week. Brock even got a new BMX bike so he can ride to school with her. They detour through the dry creek bed that curls behind the school. It's a wooded path—but not wooded enough that Cooper doesn't have to watch them bouncing along through the ruts and hear their excited chatter.

Brock, who has a voice that travels for miles, bellows, "What a *rush!*"

He's obviously trying to convince her that they have so much in common because he shares her love for extreme sports.

Even Roddy sees it from the GX-4000. "Such shameless pandering," he tut-tuts.

"It would serve him right if he breaks his neck," Cooper agrees morosely.

With a click, Roddy's ghostly form bursts out of the phone and hurtles across the field toward the woods. Cooper watches in horror as the shimmering shape swoops down on the two bikers. For an instant, the cloud encircles Brock's helmeted head.

With a cry of shock, Brock panics and slams on the brakes. The bike lurches to a halt, launching him over the handle-bars. He sails through the air and makes a three-point landing on his knees and his nose.

"Brock!" Jolie screams.

Cooper takes off across the field, high-stepping through the weeds in the direction of the fallen Brock. Halfway there, Roddy returns to the GX-4000.

"How now, Coopervega?" he says in a smug tone. "What thinkest thee of that?"

"Why would you do that?" Cooper rasps.

"It was *thy* idea," the ghost replies. "I did it to please thee."

By the time Cooper reaches the scene of the face-planting, Brock is sitting up beside his fallen bike, the helmet in his lap. His jeans are ripped at the knees and his nose is streaming crimson. Jolie has torn the first page off his script and holds it against his face like a handkerchief. It's so soaked through with blood that you can barely read the words *Romeo and Juliet, by William Shakespeare.*

"What happened?" Cooper asks. Of course, he knows exactly what happened, but there's no way Brock and Jolie could realize they've been the victims of a ghost attack.

"He lost control of the bike," Jolie explains. There are bloodstains on her YOSEMITE BUNGEE BRIGADE T-shirt.

"I didn't lose control!" Brock rages in a nasal voice. "Suddenly, there was this cloud around me and everything went all blurry!"

Cooper and Jolie look up. The sky is bright blue and utterly cloudless.

Brock becomes even more agitated. "It was a very small cloud. And it came right at me!"

"A BMX bike isn't a toy," Jolie explains. "It's a sophisticated piece of athletic equipment. If you slam on the brakes when you're going fast, you're going to throw yourself off of it."

"What do you know?" Brock demands. "It really, really hurts!"

"We've got to get him to the nurse," Jolie tells Cooper. "She'll put ice on that nose before the swelling gets too bad."

"Now Whatshisface is in on this too?" Brock's voice is even more outraged. "What are you—EMTs?"

"His caterwauling remindeth me of the mewling of an infant," Roddy comments through the earbud.

Cooper is torn. On the one hand, he has no great love for Brock—and for very good reason. On the other hand, this is Roddy's fault—done as a result of something Cooper said. Jolie, the extreme athlete, considers this just another wipe-out. It happens to her all the time, and she always bounces back. But Cooper doesn't like the amount of blood pouring out of Brock's nose, now soaking the script clear through to act 1, scene 3.

Jolie abandons her bike and she and Cooper begin walking Brock toward the school.

"Not so fast!" Brock complains. "My knees are hurt too, you know. They sting like crazy!"

For the first time, Jolie looks a little worried. As Brock's injured nose swells, his voice becomes increasingly high-pitched and nasal. When he talks about "my knees," it comes out "by dees." This is the guy who's supposed to star as Romeo in two days.

Chuckling sounds come from the earbud.

They're crossing the soccer field, leaving a trail of blood droplets, when Aiden abandons the game and comes running. "Whoa, what happened to him?"

"It was a cloud," Brock bubbles.

"A cloud of what—vampire bats?"

"More like baseball bats," puts in another soccer teammate.

"You guys are hilarious." Brock is bitter. "I'm dying and you're cracking jokes."

"*I'b dyigg,*" Roddy mimics through the earbud.

"Shhh!" Cooper hisses.

Alerted by one of the students, the nurse comes racing out of the school, Mr. Marchese hot on her heels.

"Brock!" the director exclaims at the sight of his leading man dripping blood all over the grass.

"Hi, Mr. Marchese." *Bister Barchese.*

"A cloud got him," Aiden explains tragically. "Bad."

Jolie speaks up. "It's my fault. We were BMXing to school and I forgot he's not as experienced as I am." Her eyes widen. "What if he can't play Romeo on Saturday?"

"Don't even say that out loud!" the director begs.

"I'm fine," Brock insists. *I'b fide.*

"I'll be the judge of that," the nurse insists. "I'll drive him to the hospital. That nose should be X-rayed."

CHAPTER TWENTY
LIFESAVER

The entire seventh grade is on pins and needles throughout the morning. In one split-second biking accident, a play that was well in hand and ready to go is suddenly hanging by a thread. The rumors sweep through the school like a brush fire. The cast and crew can talk of nothing else.

"What if he has to stay in the hospital?"

"What if he misses the play?"

"What if his face is messed up?"

"What if his voice is messed up?"

"Oh, this is so messed up!"

"What if he gets amnesia and forgets his lines?"

The tension hangs in the air like fog. After all their hard work for all these weeks, are they about to lose one of their stars two days before the curtain rises on *Romeo and Juliet*?

In the seventh-grade wing of Stratford Middle School, faces are taut with nervousness, lips thin and bloodless. Classes are reduced to silent reading. The teachers are too worried to teach. The principal has to sub for Mr. Marchese, who has gone to the emergency room to monitor the progress of his Romeo.

Jolie gets permission to trek out to the dry creek bed and rescue the BMX bikes. When she asks Cooper to go with her, Roddy is excited.

"Thou must tell her, Coopervega!"

"Tell her what?" Cooper growls, pulling his jacket out of his locker. "That the 'cloud' that almost killed Brock lives in my phone?"

"That thou knowest the part of Romeo," Roddy insists. "And thou art ready to replace the buffoon, whose voice be that of a sick goat."

Cooper is horrified. "Is that what this is about? You attacked Brock so I could take his part in the play? Roddy, why would you do such an awful thing?"

"In my world, we did not call them *awful things*; we called them *things*. Truly awful things we had aplenty—beheadings and hangings, stretching on the rack, and the dreaded iron maiden. But Brock is not dead, nor is he disfigured for life. He will recover—merely not in time to play Romeo. That happy task is thine for the taking—"

"No!" Cooper interrupts angrily

"And afterward," the ghost goes on, "fair Jolie will surely love thee. I am overjoyed to have been able to grant thee this favor."

Cooper is appalled. "I don't *want* this favor! Sure, Brock's a jerk, and a lousy actor besides. But he didn't deserve what you did to him!"

"Nor did I deserve the plague," Roddy replies mournfully. "Nor did my brilliant father deserve the executioner. 'Tis far from fair, this life."

"Oh, no, you don't," Cooper says harshly. "You can't blame this on fate. What happened to Brock was all you. If you'd never learned how to click yourself out of the phone, Brock wouldn't be in the emergency room having his nose tweezered out of the back of his skull. And the play would have a Romeo."

"The play *hath* a Romeo," the ghost fires back. "Thee. Thou art superior to the buffoon in every way. Who knoweth this better than I? Romeo is Barnabas, and Barnabas is my creation."

"I don't want to get a part just because the guy ahead of me got taken out by my ghost henchman. Every time I close my eyes, I see Brock, his face bashed in, gushing blood all over the place—"

"I know," comes Jolie's voice from behind him.

Cooper wheels, embarrassed. "Oh—sorry. I guess I was kind of talking to myself."

"I can't help thinking that it's partly my fault," she says sadly. "I should have gone a little slower. The BMX was new, and Brock wasn't that experienced."

"You can't blame yourself," Cooper soothes her.

No, you can blame the "cloud."

"The worst part," she goes on, "is that Brock had an

accident, and I feel bad about it, sure. But what really worries me is that we might have lost our Romeo." She looks up at Cooper. "Does that make me a terrible person?"

"That is thy cue, Coopervega," Roddy exclaims in his ear. "Thou must tell her *thou* shalt play Romeo. 'Tis verily a slam dunk!"

In answer, Cooper takes out the earbud and drops it into his pocket beside the phone. "You can't blame yourself," he repeats. "You only have one speed—full out. If he tried to match that and he wasn't ready, that's his problem."

That and ticking off the wrong ghost.

They exit the school and trek out to the accident scene in the rutted path along the dry creek bed. Jolie picks up Brock's BMX first, rolling it along the uneven ground. "It's fine," she concludes. "I wonder what went wrong. It was almost like the bike stopped and he kept on going."

"Extreme sports aren't for everybody," Cooper replies, feeling guilty—but not that guilty—for kicking Brock while he's down.

With Brock's gigantic helmet threatening to slip off his head, Cooper rides alongside Jolie, working hard to avoid the second wipeout of the day. The BMX is too big for him and the path is so rough that a ghost attack is the least of a rider's worries. He's relieved when they reach the smooth pavement of the school's driveway and secure the bikes in the rack by the main entrance.

It's just then that Mr. Marchese drives up with Brock. The boy lets himself out of the passenger door and feels for the curb with his foot. A huge ice pack obscures his entire face.

"How did it go?" asks Jolie.

The reply comes in a high-pitched nasal twang. "Dot so good." The ice pack lowers, revealing a giant bandage covering a swollen nose. Two black eyes complete the gruesome picture. "I broke by dose."

Jolie muffles a gasp and mumbles, "It's—uh—not as bad as I thought."

An obvious lie. It's ten times worse than she thought. And the most horrendous part is Brock's voice. With his face swollen, he sounds like Donald Duck speaking through a fifty-cent kazoo.

Cooper takes out his phone to show Roddy his handiwork.

"Put that away," Mr. Marchese snaps irritably. "This isn't something for you to post on Instagram!"

Even with the earbud in his pocket, Cooper can hear the ghost's distant cheering. "But," he manages, "the performance—"

"A student's health is more important than any performance," the director announces tragically.

"I cad still bake it," Brock buzzes stubbornly. *"Oh, I ab fortude's fool . . ."*

Donald Duck reciting Shakespeare through a fifty-cent kazoo.

*   *   *

Since Brock's parents are both at work, Chad swings over from the high school during his lunch period to give his injured brother a ride home. Veronica is in the car with him.

She regards Cooper suspiciously as he helps Chad load Brock's BMX into the trunk.

"What?" he demands.

She folds her arms in front of her. "Tell me what you know about this."

"Brock fell off his bike. What's to know?"

"That's not everything," she persists. "I can see it in your face."

"Look—" He sidles up to her, speaking in a low voice. "Just because you're a soccer star doesn't make you good at everything. He got pitched off and broke his nose. Even the helmet couldn't save him. It was an accident . . ."

It's no use. Cooper can feel the hot flush pouring into his cheeks. He's never been able to hide anything from Veronica.

On the way back to class, Cooper stops in the bathroom to pop the earbud back in. "Way to go, Roddy," he mutters. "Veronica thinks I know something about what happened to Brock. Which I do, but I can't tell *her* that—not if I don't want to end up in the nuthouse."

"The time is come to declare thyself," Roddy urges. "'Fear not,' thou must say. 'Behold thy new Romeo.'"

"If you don't shut up about that, I'm taking the battery out of my phone," Cooper threatens him.

"But the play—"

"The teachers will figure out what to do with the play," Cooper cuts in. "Whatever they decide, that's how it's going to go."

By the time Cooper gets back to class, word of Brock's accident has spread to every single kid. They all know that their silent reading has nothing to do with reading, and everything to do with freeing the teachers to have an emergency meeting on the status of the play.

"Brock's really messed up," Jolie tells the anxious students. "There's absolutely no way he can perform on Saturday. He looks like he lost a fight with a battering ram!"

"Oh," Aiden says in worried understanding. "That must be why Mr. Marchese ate a whole pack of Tums before going to the conference room with the other teachers."

Ruth is horrified. "You don't think they're going to cancel the play?!"

"Nah, we'll just do it without Romeo," Tyler says sarcastically. "It'll be a lot shorter, and we'll have to change the name to *Juliet*. And it might be tough explaining why she kills herself at the end—"

"Be serious," Jolie interrupts. "The teachers will have to postpone—you know, at least until Brock gets his voice back and can take that giant bandage off his poor nose."

"Coopervega—" Roddy hisses. "How doth one find this conference room?"

"Stay out of this, Roddy," Cooper mumbles under his breath.

But in answer, there's a familiar click, and Roddy's spectral form begins to rise from Cooper's pocket. Cooper falls out of his chair and sprawls onto the floor to distract attention from the ghost slipping under the door and disappearing into the hall. To his surprise, he barely gets laughed at or even noticed. The students are just too uptight. For more than a month, they have struggled to put together a difficult Shakespearean play. Could it really be coming apart two days before the performance?

Jolie and Aiden haul Cooper up and deposit him back in his chair. Cooper barely thanks them. His mind is in the conference room, frantic that the teachers don't discover that they have an eavesdropper and follow him back to his home in the GX-4000. Or worse, that Mr. Marchese might connect the dots between the shimmering specter in the conference room and the mysterious cloud that wiped out Brock on his bike.

Calm down. Cooper struggles to soothe himself. *Nobody sees Roddy because nobody's looking for a ghost. The only reason I see him is because I know he's there.*

As the minutes pass, Cooper begins to sweat. For sure, Roddy is bumping up against the longest time he's ever been outside the phone. He can't get lost, can he? At the Wolfson museum, he found his way back to a moving bus. Sooner or later, the GX-4000 always draws him in.

At that moment, the door is flung wide and Mr. Marchese enters the room, stoop-shouldered, pasty-faced, looking like he's just lost his last friend. "People, listen up. There's no easy way to say this . . ."

In a wave of shimmering air, Roddy sweeps in between the teacher's feet and leaps into Cooper's pocket. "Coopervega!" he gasps. "Thou must set this right—"

Cooper can't take his eyes off his despondent teacher.

"Some of you might know that Brock had a bicycle accident this morning," the director goes on in a resigned tone. "It means we've lost our Romeo. We tried to postpone the performance, but Mr. Wolfson's business interests take him to Asia as of next week. There's nothing we can do but cancel our play."

A chorus of protest goes up in the classroom.

"But we worked so hard!"

"We were just getting good!"

"My grandparents are driving in from Toledo just to see it!"

"We'll be the only seventh grade that never did a Shakespeare play!"

As the angry babble subsides into a melancholy silence, Cooper hears Roddy's voice through the earbud. "Tell them,

Coopervega! This is thine only chance! Do not let this opportunity be thrown out with the contents of the chamber pot!"

Cooper hisses back one word. "No!"

"Then I shall!"

Cooper hears an electronic pop—the sound of the earbud being turned off. Roddy's voice comes out of the
phone's speaker, muffled by the pocket, but shouting at top
volume:

"Coopervega can do it! He will be Romeo!"

"Who said that?" demands the teacher.

A few voices even ask, "Who's Cooper Vega?"

Oh, great, Cooper reflects. On top of it all, he's Whatshisface
again.

Aiden jumps to his feet. "That's right! Remember the
Capulets' ball? Cooper did Romeo! I'll bet he knows
the whole part!"

Mr. Marchese turns urgent eyes on his Second Watchman.
"Cooper—is this true?"

All Cooper can manage to do is nod.

"We'll try you out at rehearsal tonight. If you really do
know this role, you'll be a lifesaver!"

The class breaks into applause. Cooper catches a glowing
look from Jolie that sends his dark mood soaring.

Sometimes it's not such a terrible thing to have a ghost in
your phone.

CHAPTER TWENTY-ONE
THE ANTI-WHATSHISFACE

Cooper stands in the wings at rehearsal, frozen with fear. It's one thing to practice in the privacy of your own bedroom, with nobody to hear you but the ghost of someone who lived more than four hundred years ago. It's quite another to perform a lead role in a cast that's already been perfecting this show for weeks.

You're not Romeo, he tells himself. *You're Second Watchman. You're Whatshisface, both in the play and in real life.*

Worst of all, the guy he's replacing is the most popular kid in the entire seventh grade.

There it is—your cue. Cooper steps out onstage, his legs jelly beneath him. He opens his mouth to deliver Romeo's first line—and draws a complete blank.

Panic, ice-cold and debilitating.

And then a voice in his ear supplies the line for him: *"Is the day so young?"*

He repeats the words, praying he can muster enough volume to get them past the footlights. To his astonishment, he hears his own voice ringing with confidence and expression.

From there, the countless hours of rehearsal kick in, and he steps up to his fellow cast members, delivering Romeo's complicated speeches with power and flair. When he stumbles over the occasional line, Roddy is right there in his earpiece to supply it. He's the playwright, after all. Who knows *Romeo and Juliet* better than he does?

But those stumbles become increasingly rare as Cooper grows into his character. He isn't reciting from memory any longer. He *is* Romeo. And the skeptical looks from the other actors are turning into admiration, relief, even celebration. The play isn't ruined because of Brock's accident; it's going to be better than ever!

Soon Jolie is onstage with him—his Juliet—and she's practically glowing with approval. As they perform their parts, speaking Shakespeare's words—*Roddy's* words—a lightness takes hold in Cooper's gut, expanding outward until it fills his entire body. He could fly if he chose to. It's triumph, but it's something else too. Transformation. His days as Whatshisface are over.

When the run-through ends, the entire cast gives Cooper a spontaneous ovation.

Mr. Marchese is practically in tears. "Cooper—why didn't you tell us you were so good?"

"I don't know if I'm good," Cooper manages to stammer.

"I guess I just kind of picked it up from hearing it over and over again at rehearsal. Since I only had one line, I spent a lot of time listening to everybody else's."

With Cooper now playing Romeo, Tyler does double duty as Second Watchman in act 5, since his character, Mercutio, dies early on in the story.

"You're fantastic," Aiden assures him. "Way better than—um, I mean—you know, not everybody could be as good as you."

What they all want to say is that he's way better than Brock, but no one comes out with the name of the former Romeo. Sidelined or not, Brock is still a major presence at Stratford Middle School. There's sympathy for the ill timing of his injury, but mostly, no one wants to get on his bad side. In spite of this, there's unspoken agreement that not only has the play been saved, it's also been improved. And by a former Whatshisface, no less.

When the directors send everybody home for dinner break that day, Cooper and Jolie leave the gym side by side. Even more impressive, Jolie walks her BMX bike so she and Cooper can discuss their upcoming roles at Saturday's performance.

"I love how you do the balcony scene," Jolie enthuses. "You really *get* that when Juliet asks 'Wherefore art thou?' she doesn't mean *where*, she means *why*—why did she have to fall for the son of her family's enemy?"

Cooper is torn in two. On one hand, he finally has Jolie all to himself, costarring with her in the most romantic story in history. He's never going to be able to keep up with her at skydiving and her extreme sports, so acting together is as good as it gets. She's impressed by his performance—and not just her. Mr. Marchese and the teachers are practically gaga over how he stepped in and saved the production. The other kids practically break into applause every time he says a line better than Brock used to say it.

If this keeps up, he'll be famous in the seventh grade—the anti-Whatshisface. It's paradise. It's perfect. But—

He can't keep his mind off the source of all this amazing luck—the "accident" that was no accident. Roddy deliberately knocked Brock out of the play—and broke the poor kid's nose in the process. If Roddy were a living person and not a ghost, he'd be guilty of assault!

How can I enjoy all this good stuff, knowing where it comes from?

In front of Cooper's house, Jolie turns to him again. "You're the best, Cooper! Our play would be in ruins if it wasn't for you."

"See you after dinner." He can't resist adding, *"Parting is such sweet sorrow."*

She regards him with such admiration that he hates himself for loving it so much. She climbs on the BMX and pedals off.

The exchange is not unnoticed by the ghost in Cooper's phone. "Ah, Coopervega, success is sweet, is it not? My advice to thee is to marry her in all haste, ere she changeth her mind."

Instead of answering, Cooper enters the house, marches straight to the kitchen, pulls a roll of masking tape out of the utility drawer, and places a piece squarely over the camera lens on the GX-4000.

"What dost thou do? And why?"

Cooper pastes a second piece of tape over the rear-facing camera, eliciting another cry of outrage from the ghost.

"Coopervega—thou hast blinded me! And—and—" There's a click, but Roddy's shimmering form does not emerge from the phone. With both lenses blocked, the ghost is trapped inside.

Roddy is deeply wounded. "I understand not. Why hast thou imprisoned me thus?"

"So you can't jump out of my phone, fly into some poor kid's face, and practically kill him like you did with Brock!" Cooper hisses.

Roddy's eyes are wide with bewilderment. "But I did that for *thee*."

"It might have been okay in your century, but people who do that now are called criminals, and they get locked up," Cooper tries to explain. "So I'm locking you inside my phone so you can't get out and do me any more 'favors.'"

"But, Coopervega—I have delivered unto thee all thy heart desires."

"Yeah, and every time I try to be happy about it, I see Brock with his bashed-in face and two black eyes. I have what my heart desires because you stole it away from Brock!"

Roddy's voice is shaky. "Are we no longer friends?"

"It's *because* we're friends that I have to stop you," Cooper reasons. "Look, I know you're trying to help, but what you did was totally out of control. I have a responsibility to the other people in my century to protect them from you."

"But, Coopervega—"

"Now I'm taking the earbud out so we can both cool off. I'll get back to you after the play and we can figure out how to go on from there."

On the way to after-dinner rehearsal, Jolie has an idea. "Let's stop by Brock's house and check in on how he's feeling."

"Well," Cooper hedges, "we don't want to be late . . ."

"We won't stay long," Jolie promises. "We'll just say, you know, we're thinking of him."

Oh, I'm thinking of him, all right, Cooper reflects. *Thanks to him, I'm at war with a ghost.*

"Besides," Jolie adds, "it'll be a boost to the rest of the cast to know that Brock is doing okay."

At the Bumgartner home, Brock's mother ushers them

into the living room, where her son is on the couch, propped up on so many cushions that he reminds Cooper of "The Princess and the Pea." If anything, he looks even worse than he did when they saw him last. His black eyes have bloomed into multicolored splashes of modern art, and the tops of his cheeks have swollen in sympathy with his nose.

Spying Jolie, he beams, which is a gruesome sight. Then he notices Cooper. "How cub you brought Whatshisface?"

"Hi, Brock," Cooper manages. "It's good to see you doing so—well."

"I'b dot doigg well," Brock replies nasally. "I'b dyigg."

"I know you're worried about what's going to happen to the play," Jolie trills, beaming at him. "Well, we've got great news. Cooper is taking over Romeo."

"Wherefore art me," Cooper adds, repeating Brock's signature joke.

Brock's face darkens, which is quite a feat, considering most of it is pretty dark already. It's plain that if he could frown, he would.

Chad appears in the living room, Veronica in tow. "We're going out to the diner. Should I bring you back a sub?"

"I cad't chew," his injured kid brother laments.

"One pea soup coming up," Chad replies cheerily. "No crackers. Come on, V. I'm starving."

"Feel better, Brock," Veronica says with an accusing look at Cooper.

"We should go too," puts in Jolie. "We just wanted to say hi and let you know that your part's in good hands."

The sound that comes from Brock is like an old car with a broken muffler.

When the door shuts behind them, Veronica pulls her younger brother aside as Jolie walks ahead. "Real classy, Cooper—coming over here with Brock's girl to rub it in his face that you stole his part."

"First of all, she isn't Brock's girl," Cooper returns. "She isn't anybody's girl. And I didn't *steal* his part. I just happened to be the only other person who knows it. What am I supposed to do? Make them cancel the play? Zounds!"

She stares at him. "Zounds?"

"Yeah, *zounds*! It's a Shakespeare word." More to the point, it's a Roddy word. Is the ghost's language starting to seep into Cooper's everyday speech?

"Let's go, Cooper!" Jolie calls. "Rehearsal in five minutes."

The two of them run off toward school.

CHAPTER TWENTY-TWO
SILENCE

The quiet is hard to get used to.

For weeks, Roddy's voice has been a constant companion. With the earbud, it's almost as if the ghost can speak directly into Cooper's brain. Sometimes, it's hard to tell the difference between Roddy's words and Cooper's own thoughts.

And now . . . silence.

Of course, Roddy hasn't been silent. The earbud in Cooper's pocket worked overtime until he remembered to turn it off. The difference is that—on or off—Cooper is ignoring it. He feels guilty about it, even sad, but it's what he has to do. He's always known that the ghost's presence inside the phone is a paranormal occurrence. But until the attack on Brock, he never realized how *dangerous* Roddy could be. Friend or no, Roddy is a supernatural being who doesn't belong in the twenty-first century. And the fact that he doesn't understand that he did anything wrong only underscores the danger.

Cooper realizes he's just putting off the problem. Tomorrow, when the seventh graders take their final bow at the end of *Romeo and Juliet,* he will still have a ghost in his phone, and he will have to figure out what to do about that. The danger of Roddy will not disappear. For all Cooper knows, it might even get worse. Roddy has already taught himself how to pop in and out of the phone at will, and to stay in the real world for longer and longer periods. Who knows what he might learn next? Cooper believes with all his heart that Roddy is not a bad person, and whatever harm he does is not truly evil. But maybe that can change too.

With the earbud off and the GX-4000's volume on zero, Roddy's voice has been muted. One positive benefit: Cooper doesn't have to worry about the ghost distracting him while he's trying to act. But it also means Roddy won't be there to prompt him if Cooper forgets a line. Having the playwright himself inside your head is a powerful resource.

By this time, though, Cooper's mastery of Romeo's part is 100 percent. He won't need Roddy's help. He won't need anybody's.

Still, throughout the dress rehearsals on Friday, Cooper can't help checking on the ghost every now and then to make sure he's all right—if that can ever be said about someone who's been dead for over four hundred years. Roddy's always there—where else would he be with the masking tape trapping him inside the phone? His mouth is moving, his expression pleading. His gestures are increasingly agitated.

Cooper feels terrible, but he has to stay strong—at least until the play is over.

On Friday night, the final run-through is a huge success. The actors deliver their lines crisply, and no one stumbles over the unfamiliar Shakespearean language. At this point, they've been rehearsing so long that the words come naturally to them—the *forsooth*s, the *verily*s, and the *methinks*es. The costumes have been altered and tweaked; everything fits perfectly. The crew expertly rolls the large set pieces on and off the stage. And the lighting changes happen easily and flawlessly.

When the narrator speaks the final words, cast and crew flood the stage. Cooper and Jolie are yanked up from their funeral slabs and battered with high fives and backslaps of congratulations.

For Cooper, the transformation is complete. It stretches far beyond just the play. In the halls at school, on the street, in town, he gets a friendly wave and a "Hi, Cooper!" That's never happened anywhere else, much less in Stratford. Sixth graders treat him like a hero. Eighth graders talk to him. He *belongs*—something an army brat doesn't experience very often.

He's Romeo, but he's something more. He's Cooper.

Mr. Marchese is all smiles. "Excellent work, people! If we can replicate this performance tomorrow, we'll knock Mr.

Wolfson's socks off. And obviously," he adds as an after-thought, "your families', neighbors', and friends'."

Even on the walk home, when she's traded Juliet's gown for a CAPE CANAVERAL SPACE CAMP T-shirt, Jolie is still glowing. "One time, we went skiing in Utah," she raves. "When my dad wasn't looking, I went over this jump. There I was, high above the mountain, catching air. I could even see my dad, pointing at me and yelling—what a thrill!"

"What was your dad yelling?" Cooper asks.

"*You're grounded, missy!*" She giggles. "And I was—for a month. But it was totally worth it. Well, that's how I feel about this play. When I'm out there onstage, it's just as much of a rush."

"It's a rush for me too," Cooper tells her. It's not exactly true. But since they're never going to share the ski jump, they might as well share the acting.

"You're amazing, Cooper," she says emotionally. "The way you stepped in and took over Romeo—our play would never be this good if . . ." Her voice trails off, and he can tell she feels disloyal to the *last* Romeo—the one who would be standing in Cooper's shoes right now if Roddy hadn't taken matters into his ghostly hands.

"Brock would have been really great too," Cooper offers generously. Another lie, but it seems like the right thing to say.

Jolie reaches out and hugs him, squeezing just a little bit

longer than he expects—a whole Mississippi and a half, maybe two. He's hyperaware of the sequin stars on her shirt pressing against him.

"You're a good person, Cooper," she says. Then she runs off toward home, leaving him standing on his front walk, grinning like he's lost his mind.

His first impulse is to tell Roddy, which brings him back to earth with a sobering thud. Roddy should hear about a lot of things. Cooper and Jolie. The last dress rehearsal. The ghost deserves to know about the play more than anybody. It's *his* play—most of it.

Cooper lets himself into the house. His parents are in the living room. They ask him a few questions about rehearsal, but they're more interested in the movie they're watching. Veronica's on a date with Chad, no big surprise. They're probably out buying smoothies or baby food so Brock won't starve to death.

Upstairs in his room, Cooper stares at the four walls. He suddenly feels as lonely as he's ever been. It makes no sense. Who spends more time alone than Cooper, who changes towns and schools as often as some people change their socks? He can't count the number of places he's lived where he was gone before making a single friend. This is different. He *has* friends; he might even be on the way to a girlfriend. He's at the very center of the biggest thing in the seventh grade—the annual Shakespeare play. He could complain about loneliness in those other towns, but not here. Sure, it was a rocky start in Stratford, but the transformation from Whatshisface to Romeo is complete. So what's the problem?

He thinks about it a second more, and the answer comes easily. In the beginning, when there was no one else, there was the ghost of Roderick Northrop. No town, no play, no friend or even girlfriend can replace that.

He pulls the GX-4000 from his pocket and watches numbly as the worn piece of masking tape comes off the rear camera and flutters to the floor. Before Cooper is able to process what this might mean, he hears the click.

Roddy's spectral form explodes out of the phone and circles the room at dizzying speed just below the ceiling.

"Roddy—" Cooper breathes.

The ghost slows just enough to glare at him before swooping low and disappearing through the crack under the door. Cooper barrels into the hall in time to see Roddy streak down the steps, darting like lightning through every room in the house.

"What was that?" Mrs. Vega asks from the living room.

"Probably just a moth," her husband assures her. "I'll get a magazine and teach it some manners."

Heart pounding, Cooper races downstairs, although he's not sure what he plans to do when he comes face-to-face with the ghost. It's not as if he can catch Roddy with a butterfly net. He might as well be chasing moonbeams.

Outside the kitchen, his father hands him a copy of *National Geographic.* "If you see a giant moth, clobber it."

Cooper nods dizzily. At the moment, the "moth" is sitting on a blade of the ceiling fan, shaking his fist at them. Cooper shoots him a pleading gesture, but Roddy is too angry to be reasonable. He streaks across the front hall and disappears through the mail slot.

Cooper fights off the impulse to run outside and chase him through the neighborhood. He'd never be able to explain *that* to his parents—not at ten-thirty at night.

He does the only sensible thing. He goes back upstairs to his room, opens the window a crack, and sits on the edge of his bed with the phone in his hand. Sooner or later, the ghost will be drawn back into the GX-4000. All Cooper has to do is wait.

There's no telling how long that will take. It's gone way beyond counting Mississippis. A full twenty minutes has passed when Roddy's shimmering figure is finally wrenched in under the window sash and slammed into the phone.

Almost immediately, there's another click. But Cooper is expecting it, and already has his thumb blocking the rear camera. "Roddy—wait!"

The ghost appears on the screen—wild-eyed, disheveled, and out of breath. "Release me!" he demands in a frantic tone.

"Not till we talk this out!"

"Thou hast betrayed my trust," Roddy accuses, "after I meant thee nothing but good."

"I know. I'm sorry. It's just"—Cooper struggles to find the right words—"your century and mine . . . they don't mix. I totally get that you were only trying to help."

The ghost does not reply, but he's listening. Cooper forges on. "I'm going to let go of the lens now, but you have to promise to stay with me, okay?"

He removes his thumb from the lens. There's no click. Roddy is still there. Cooper sighs with relief. "Thanks for trusting me."

"What choice have I?" Roddy returns bitterly. "'Tis never long before this phone of thine draweth me back to my prison."

"That's what we have to talk about," Cooper tells him. "I know it's not fair, but we're stuck together—you to the phone, and me to you."

"Thou hast my most sincere sympathy." Sarcasm drips from the ghost's words. "Thou livest in a world of marvels, with a mother and a father who care for thee. Food dost thou taste, and the cool wind bloweth through thy abundant hair. And I? There is no down, no up. I am not dead; neither do I live. Would that my brilliant father had never invented this vile device thou callest a phone."

"He didn't, Roddy. The telephone was invented by a guy named Alexander Graham Bell."

Roddy is stubborn. "Thou hast just explained my purpose in this strange place. I must reclaim the reputation of my illustrious sire from thieves like this Alexander Graham Bell! Where is he that I might confront him?"

Cooper shakes his head. "It's no good. He died a long time ago."

"As did I," the ghost points out.

"Yeah, but he isn't in anybody's phone—at least, I don't think so. Listen, Roddy, you're probably going to hate me for saying this, but it's the truth: You're not here to reclaim your father's reputation, because your father doesn't have a reputation to reclaim. He didn't invent any of the things you say he did—not the TV, not the school bus, not even the garden gnome. He hasn't been forgotten; nobody knew about him in the first place. I'm sure he was a great dad, but that's all he was. To believe that you're here to get justice for him is nuts. It would make just as much sense—more, really—if the person who needed justice was—was—"

When the idea forms in Cooper's mind, he's so shocked that he falls silent right in the middle of the sentence.

Roddy is white-faced and tight-lipped on the small screen. "Please go on, Coopervega. There is still my mother thou hast not yet insulted. And perhaps my grandparents, though I knew them not—"

"Roddy—" Cooper's voice is breathless with urgency. "What if you're not here to fix your *dad's* reputation? What if you're here to fix your own?"

"What reputation have I?" Roddy asks resentfully. "I am but a poor boy, too soon an orphan, too soon a corpse."

"You're the true author of one of the most famous plays ever written," Cooper persists. "Shakespeare ripped it off, but that doesn't change the fact that it's yours."

"And a fat lot I can do about that," the ghost laments. "Shakespeare is as dead as I. He hath not a BMX bicycle from whence to unseat him."

"Forget Shakespeare. He's out of reach." Cooper's excitement is rising. "What if the reason you're here is to claim the credit that was stolen from you? Maybe it's not a coincidence that, out of all the phones in the world, you ended up in mine—a kid whose school is doing *Romeo and Juliet*. And in the very same town where your original manuscript is locked away in a secret room in The Wolf's museum."

"Thy argument hath merit," Roddy concedes, suddenly engaged. "What is thy plan that I shall be credited as the author of *Barnabas and Ursula*?"

"I'll talk to Mr. Wolfson," Cooper decides. "When he's at school for the play. I'll tell him we know about the manuscript and demand that he show it to the world. It'll be in your handwriting, not Shakespeare's, which will *prove*—"

"It will prove nothing," the ghost cuts in, "because The Wolf will reveal it to no one. Why should he? Thou art but a boy, no older than was I when the plague bore me off and vile Shakespeare presented my play as his own."

Cooper nods glumly. "So we're right back where we started from."

"Coopervega—dost thou not see?" the ghost crows. "*We* must remove *Barnabas and Ursula* from the museum! No man can deny its meaning when he beholdeth it with his own eyes."

Cooper is appalled. "That's stealing!"

"Nay," Roddy reasons. "It was stolen from me. It was stolen from the world when The Wolf locked it away. But I cannot steal what is rightfully mine."

"It doesn't matter," Cooper tells him. "The Wolf has millions of dollars' worth of stuff in that museum. No way does he leave the place open for anybody to waltz in and help themselves. There are employees, guards, probably a burglar alarm."

"'Twas no trouble for me," Roddy points out.

"Because you're a *cloud*. Besides, what good is it for you to get in there? You can't pick up the manuscript and run off with it. You need me for that. And I don't fit through keyholes or under doors. A trained security guy is going to notice me standing there, trying to pick the lock."

"No need to concern thyself with such insignificant details," the ghost exclaims, inspired. "Thou shalt have with thee the son of the greatest scientific mind of the sixteenth century. With my father's genius, we shall devise a strategy that is quick and simple and foolproof."

"No way, Roddy. You're a ghost—there's nothing solid about you that they can throw in jail. *I'm* the one who's going to get arrested for breaking into Mr. Wolfson's museum."

"It will not happen," Roddy assures him. "We are the perfect team, thou and I. Thou shalt be my hands, as I cannot grasp. And I shall be thine eyes to warn thee of any approaching danger."

Cooper is unconvinced. "There must be some other way. Maybe I should go to the police—they could order The Wolf to hand over the manuscript. Or my dad—he has all kinds of contacts in the military."

"Thou hast already concluded thou would not be believed," Roddy reminds him. "And if I am revealed, thou hast warned that scientists would dismantle the phone, leaving me— where? This is the only way."

Cooper stares at the ghost's pleading expression on the screen. This relic of a bygone era honestly expects him to go out and commit grand larceny. Unbelievable! And yet, it's still not half as unbelievable as the simple reality that Roddy's in the phone in the first place. How can anything be expected to make sense when that's what you're starting out with?

The facts, crazy as they are, whirl around Cooper's head as he struggles to put them together in some kind of logical order. Roddy, his stolen play, and the proof of it, locked away in the Wolfson museum. If Cooper's right, and Roddy's purpose in the twenty-first century is to claim credit for *Romeo and Juliet,* how can Cooper deny him the help that he needs?

"Coopervega—I beg you," the ghost pleads. "By our friendship—"

That's what settles it for Cooper. As impossible as all this sounds, one thing makes perfect sense: The two of them are friends. And friends don't let each other down.

"All right," he says. "What do I have to do?"

CHAPTER TWENTY-THREE

FOURTEEN MINUTES AND ELEVEN SECONDS

Curtain time for *Romeo and Juliet* is at one p.m. Call for the cast is at eleven-thirty. That's when costumes will be put on, makeup will be applied, and last-minute pep talks will be delivered. Every second of the past six weeks of rehearsal has been building up to this moment—showtime.

Soon Stratford Middle School will be a beehive of activity, the center of the local universe. Shortly after nine a.m., however, the building is deserted except for two people in the chemistry lab. Actually, one person and one ghost.

An assortment of beakers, test tubes, and stoppered bottles is spread out across the experiment table.

"I hope you know what you're doing, Roddy," Cooper says dubiously. "If this is another one of your brimstone stink bombs, remember that the whole town is going to be here in a few hours. We've worked too hard and too long to have *Romeo and Juliet* canceled because of rotten-egg smell."

"Fear not," Roddy soothes via the earbud. "This formula calls for no brimstone."

"Yeah, well, the fumes are pretty nasty, just the same." Wincing, Cooper waves the eyedropper under his nose.

A tiny bubble of liquid squeezes out of the opening and hits the table. With a hissing sound and a wisp of smoke, the liquid eats into the countertop, creating a divot half an inch deep.

"Roddy!" Cooper exclaims in horror. "Something's wrong! You broke the school again!"

"Nothing is wrong, Coopervega," the ghost assures him. "This is the mixture's purpose. When the constables arrested my father, I would follow him to their jails. Just a droplet of this powerful acid burneth through the locks, and he would be free."

"The question is, will it burneth through the bottle?" Cooper asks warily. "Because then it would just as easily burneth through my hand!"

"Fear not," Roddy reassures him, "for glass is immune to the acid's effects. That is why the mixture was so well suited to my father's purposes—and to ours this day."

Holding the bottle gingerly between two nerveless fingers, Cooper slides it into the side pocket of his backpack.

He puts away the chemicals, powders, and equipment, carefully cleaning up after himself. Shrugging into the pack, he steps out of the science room . . . and very nearly comes face-to-face with Mr. Marchese, who is striding purposefully down the hall.

Midstep, Cooper executes an emergency one-eighty and stumbles back into the lab, flattening himself against the wall. Stupid, stupid, stupid not to anticipate that *Romeo and Juliet's* director would be extra early on show day. How will Cooper ever explain what he's doing at school more than two hours before call time? Especially if Mr. Marchese notices the crater in the middle of the experiment table!

Cooper holds his breath as the director approaches. The footsteps on the terrazzo floor grow louder until they're practically gunshots. Mr. Marchese marches past the lab and continues on down the hall in the direction of the gym.

Stunned with relief, Cooper peers through the doorway at his teacher's receding back. The man's head is down and he's walking quickly. He's so focused on today's play that he didn't notice one of his stars in the wrong place at the wrong time.

"Is something the matter, Coopervega?" comes Roddy's voice in his ear. "Thy breathing is not natural to thee."

Cooper waits for the director to disappear through the heavy gym doors at the end of the hall before replying, "It's—nothing. Everything's okay."

How could he ever explain his trepidation? If he can't even

make it in and out of the science lab without coming within a hair of being caught, how can he expect to pull off the heist of the century, stealing a priceless manuscript from a billion-aire's maximum-security museum?

On the lookout for other early-bird teachers, Cooper stealthily leaves the school and gets on his bike. The Wolfson property isn't far to drive, but it's a major effort when you're pedaling, especially on the rolling terrain of the town that used to be Three Hills. Forty-five minutes have passed—and Cooper is bathed in sweat—before the majestic wrought-iron gates heave into view.

Short of the entrance to the estate, Cooper veers off the road, tires crunching on the gravel of the shoulder. He stashes the bike in the cover of the woods and pulls the GX-4000 from his pocket. "All right, Roddy, here's your first scouting mission." He taps the screen, and the image search page for keywords *surveillance camera* appears. "We need to know if there's anything that looks like one of these on the Wolfson property. It could be high up, attached to a wall, or maybe a tree. And also this." He changes the key-words to *motion detector*, and a new set of pictures is displayed. "Got it?"

"I understand." With a click, the ghost rises from the phone and sails over the gate onto the grounds of the estate. At first, Cooper can make out Roddy's shimmering features scanning the property below. Soon, though, his spectral form disappears into the brilliant sunshine.

The ghost is only gone for a few minutes, but to Cooper it feels like hours. The reality of what he's about to do is starting to sink in, and it's giving him stomach cramps. The downside of partnering with Roddy is that, during the planning stage, it's all *we* and *us*. But if anything goes wrong, that *us* turns into 100 percent *me*. Nobody's going to arrest a ghost and march him off to juvenile hall.

And there's nothing he can do to help me if it happens, because they don't allow phones in jail.

Cooper is still twisting and turning the what-ifs when Roddy returns to the phone. "Methinks thou art good to go. Cameras there are many, but with stealth, thou mayest avoid them. I shall instruct thee."

Cooper squares his shoulders and takes a deep breath for courage. "So that's it, then. Are you ready?"

"I have been ready for four hundred years," the ghost replies solemnly.

The wrought-iron gate is twenty feet high, but the stone wall that surrounds the property is only five. Cooper scrambles over that, and sets out for the E-shaped palace that houses the Wolfson Collection. Every step toward the building feels like a trip into quicksand. His footsteps reverberate with the word *Why?* in his head.

"Rightward ho," Roddy advises through the earbud. "A camera is nigh."

Cooper adjusts his course, crouching low along a neatly sculpted hedge. As he passes the mansion, he's terrified to think The Wolf is in there somewhere. A powerful man who got a whole town to change its name and probably won't take kindly to the idea of having his greatest treasures plundered by a twelve-year-old kid. A classic Rolls-Royce Corniche is parked on the circular drive. The car, Cooper notes, will soon be taking Mr. Wolfson to the middle school for *Romeo and Juliet.* That is, assuming Romeo isn't in prison by curtain time.

A quarter mile farther down the lane, the museum beckons. Cooper can see the Globe Theatre replica behind it, and as he approaches, he can make out another of the many security cameras at the main entrance. He isn't worried about that—the front door was never part of their plan. Their destination: the far side of the building, out of view of The Wolf's mansion.

"Thou art rocking, Coopervega," Roddy's voice sounds in his ear.

"We're there," Cooper agrees tensely, rounding the corner of the museum. He shrugs out of his backpack and sets it down in front of a low window. "Time to go to work."

With a click, Roddy is out of the phone again. The ghost

does a quick circle to get his bearings, and then squeezes in through a tiny space between the frame and the brick. A second later, Roddy's spectral form is bobbing on the opposite side of the glass, grinning and flashing him a thumbs-up. Then he's gone on another scouting mission, swooping through the endless museum galleries.

Cooper cools his heels, trying to remain calm. He'd feel a lot more comfortable if Roddy didn't seem to be having so much fun on this expedition. Then again, the poor guy didn't have much going on for the past four centuries, so he can't be blamed for strutting his stuff a little.

Roddy is back quickly. "Evil tidings, Coopervega," he reports breathlessly. "There is a watchman and he cometh this way."

As if on cue, a uniformed security guard—an overweight man with a bushy mustache—enters the gallery, twirling a heavy key ring around his index finger. Cooper drops to his knees underneath the window. The hefty man crosses the gallery, glancing with very little interest at the displays from the English town of Stratford-upon-Avon, where Shakespeare was born and later retired after his career in the London theater. He pauses at the doorway, gives a brief final survey of the room, and moves on to the next gallery.

"He is gone!" Roddy exclaims. "Now is the moment to begin!"

"Not yet," Cooper whispers. "Let's see how long it takes him to make a circuit of the whole museum and come back here. Then we'll know how much time we have."

"Thou hast great wisdom," Roddy approves with surprise. "'Tis clear why fair Jolie prefereth thee over that lummox."

"No," Cooper replies bitterly. "She prefereth me because you threw the lummox off his bike and bashed his face in." He sets the phone on stopwatch mode and starts the counter.

The wait seems endless. It's doubly agonizing since Cooper knows he has a forty-five-minute bike ride back to town, where he's due at school for the eleven-thirty cast call. Yet he also understands that it's a good thing. It just might give them a decent amount of time to break into the secret gallery, jack Roddy's manuscript, and get out of the building before the big man comes around again.

Cooper's eyes are on the small screen as the chronometer numbers roll higher. When the security guard reappears in the gallery, Cooper halts the timer. The stopwatch shows fourteen minutes and eleven seconds.

"We can do this, Coopervega!" Roddy exclaims. "There is ample time."

Cooper swallows hard. Ample, maybe. But not a second to spare.

He sets the timer back to zero and restarts it. Fourteen minutes. The clock is ticking.

He examines the window, taking note of the tiny wire emerging from the brick and disappearing into the frame. An alarm? Probably—triggered when anybody tries to open the sash. Luckily, Cooper has prepared for that possibility, thanks to all the cop dramas Roddy has been watching on TV.

Nestling the GX-4000 in the branches of a bush so the ghost can watch, Cooper unzips his backpack and draws out the toilet plunger from the downstairs bathroom at home. Dampening the rim with a moist wipe, he holds it firmly against the glass and pushes until, with a slurping sound, it sticks.

"A device of infinite utility," Roddy approves from his vantage point. "Not merely doth it help chamber pots to empty themselves. Its purposes are truly beyond limit."

"This is the important part." From a smaller compartment, Cooper removes a pen-size glass cutter, giving silent thanks for his father's bottomless toolbox. Cooper used to scoff at Captain Vega's belief that "everything comes in handy sooner or later." Not anymore.

Focusing all his strength into maintaining a steady hand, he digs the blade into the glass and draws it across the window, following the inside of the metal frame. It's hard work, and sweat trickles into his stinging eyes as he cuts a large rectangular panel. Then, using the plunger, he draws the glass out of the window.

No alarm sounds. As far as any security system can tell, the window is untouched. Frame and sash are exactly as they were before.

"How now!" Roddy enthuses.

Throwing the backpack over his shoulder, Cooper picks up the phone and steps in through the opening in the window. He originally planned to replace the glass panel, but that would take too much time. A quick glance at the stopwatch on the phone reveals that he's already down to ten minutes.

"Make haste!" the ghost urges.

Following the direction of the security guard's circuit, Cooper moves from room to room through the half-light of the closed museum until he reaches the gallery where the first folios are displayed. There it is, on the interior wall— the door Roddy penetrated during the seventh-grade field trip. The one leading to the secret collection.

Cooper checks the GX-4000: 8:42 left.

Unable to contain himself, the ghost bursts out of the phone and disappears in through the keyhole. He's back in a matter of seconds, though, his voice quivering in excitement. "'Tis there, Coopervega, just as before! My *Barnabas and Ursula*! Thou hast but to enter and claim it!"

Just standing in the museum, knowing there's a guard around somewhere, is twisting Cooper's stomach in knots of terror. *Calm down!* he exhorts himself. *You've worked this out! You have more than eight minutes . . .*

From the backpack's side pocket he removes the small bottle of acid. He unscrews the dropper, sucks up some liquid, and fits the glass tip into the keyhole. Breathing a silent prayer, he squeezes the bulb.

A faint sizzling sound comes from inside the lock. A wisp of smoke wafts out of the keyhole. He tries the knob. It doesn't budge.

"How long before it burns through the lock?" he whispers.

"Merely an instant," Roddy replies via the earbud.

Cooper twists at the knob again. Zero movement.

"Introduce more of the acid," the ghost urges.

This time Cooper fills the dropper completely and empties the entire contents into the lock. More smoke, more sizzle. But the doorknob still won't turn.

"Curious" is Roddy's opinion. "It hath never failed before."

"Yeah—on sixteenth-century locks!" Cooper hisses. "They've learned a few things in the past four hundred years. Like how to make them acid-proof. Progress hasn't been all school buses and chamber pots, you know!" He barely stops himself from slapping his forehead in dismay—which would have emptied the rest of the bottle over his head. Yikes! Maybe the acid can't open locks, but it would have little trouble burning through his skull down into his brain.

Desperate now—the stopwatch shows under four minutes—Cooper tries one more dropperful of acid. Same result—none at all. In a last-ditch effort, he heaves his shoulder into the door, hoping that the weakened lock might give way. Nothing.

And then a deep voice calls, "Is someone there?"

CHAPTER TWENTY-FOUR
THE FORBIDDEN GALLERY

There's no time to run. All Cooper can do is throw himself behind one of the display cases and pray that the big man doesn't notice him.

The guard runs onto the scene, panting with exertion. "Who's there?"

Cooper holds his breath, trying his best to be absolutely still. But even as he hunkers there, he realizes that his cause is hopeless. In a room this size, the guy would have to be blind to miss him.

He's keeping so silent that the all-too-familiar click seems as loud as a bomb blast. Roddy's spectral form rises from the GX-4000 and heads for the guard like a guided missile.

What's he doing? Cooper asks himself. *He can't fight that guy! He can't even touch him!*

Cooper risks a glance up from the floor. The big guard is frozen like a statue, his eyes wide with fright. He looks— he looks—

Like he's seeing a ghost!

In the half-light of the museum, Roddy's shimmering figure is perfectly visible, hovering in the air before the terrified man, leering and making threatening gestures.

Cooper reacts on pure instinct. He cups his hands to his mouth and booms in the scariest voice he can muster, *"I am the ghost of William Shakespeare!"*

The guard's wide eyes roll back in his head, and he crumples to the floor, out cold.

Cooper rushes to the fallen security man. He's unconscious, but still breathing.

Roddy jumps back into the phone. "Begone, Coopervega! Thou must abandon this folly!"

"Roddy, wait—"

"He will awaken soon!" the ghost warns. "Risk not thy future for—"

But Cooper has already seen it—the key ring still clutched in the man's hand. He fishes it out of the limp fingers and rushes over to the door to the secret room.

"Bravo!" Roddy applauds. "Thou art brilliant!"

Cooper begins fumbling with one key after another, hoping against hope that Alistair Northrop's acid hasn't ruined the lock for good and always. Finally, on the sixth try, the cylinder turns and the door swings wide.

Cooper feels a jolt of exhilaration as he enters the billionaire's forbidden gallery. He's expecting an exhibit even more elaborate and fancy for The Wolf's most prized possessions, yet this room is smaller and spare, dimly lit, with items displayed on simple shelves and tables. There are manuscript pages under glass, handwritten letters, and what look like legal documents. There are articles of clothing in rich fabrics and several pairs of spectacles. There's even a human tooth and a certificate of authenticity, claiming it to be Shakespeare's.

Cooper reminds himself that most of what's here are things Mr. Wolfson can't admit to owning, because they were either stolen or purchased illegally.

"Hurry up, Roddy, where is it? Where's *Barnabas and Ursula?*"

Roddy leaves the GX-4000 and flies straight to a covered glass case that appears to hold the place of honor in the secret collection. He points it out with translucent fingers.

Cooper stares at the manuscript on display. The paper is thick, uneven, and yellowed with age. The ink is faded, almost gone in places. Cooper reads the opening lines, now so famous as a part of *Romeo and Juliet*: *Two households, both alike in dignity . . .*

The penmanship is flowery, like in most of the handwritten documents from that period. Yet there's something childlike about it too—a little shakiness, a few uneven lines, the occasional inkblot. It's not hard to believe this is the work of thirteen-year-old Roddy Northrop.

Amazing. Not that Cooper ever doubted Roddy's

authorship claim. But to have the proof right in front of him at last is an electrifying experience. He looks up at Roddy's hovering form and sees pride in the shimmering features.

What a genius Roddy must have been—and still must be. A London street kid, with no mother and a flaky father who was constantly in trouble with the law—apprenticed to a cruel printer with an aloof daughter who never so much as glanced in Roddy's direction. He had zero luck, no breaks, and very little kindness from anyone. And before the plague put an end to his short life, he managed to write a classic play that most people consider the greatest romance of all time.

Cooper reaches for the glass top, assuming it's locked. It wouldn't be the first glass he's broken today, yet his preference is to leave the museum as undamaged as possible. But no—the glass cover opens easily. He takes hold of the thick manuscript and lifts it off the velvet base.

An alarm goes off—a blaring klaxon that fills the museum with its repeating roar. Roddy's ghostly hands cover his ghostly ears, and his spectral form glows red with the flashing lights of the security system. He dives back into the phone and hollers, "Run, Coopervega!"

No command has ever been less necessary. Cooper crams the manuscript into his backpack and races out of the secret room. He nearly trips over the husky guard, who is just sitting up, rubbing his eyes, awakened by the sudden noise.

"Hey! Stop, you!"

Cooper hears heavy footfalls behind him as the man gives chase. It lends Cooper's feet wings. He sprints through the artifacts and folios and dives for the opening he cut in the window. The top of his backpack gets hung up on the frame, and he twists around, frantically reaching to free it. At last, he tumbles out of the building, nearly impaling himself on the handle of the toilet plunger, which is still attached to the panel of cut glass. For an insane instant, he actually considers stopping his escape to rescue the plunger—his father will certainly notice its absence. But then the angry guard stomps into view at the window. There's just no time.

Cooper sprints along the roadway, heading for the main gate, and beyond it, his bike. He doesn't bother to stick to the cover of the bushes now. Hiding isn't an option. People are going to notice he's been here—mostly because of the crazed security guard and the howling alarm klaxon. Speed is all that matters.

He makes only one detour—to the parked Rolls-Royce on the mansion's circular driveway. Heart hammering, he throws off the backpack and fishes in the side pocket.

"Why dost thou pause?" Roddy demands through the earbud. "Thou must bust a move!"

"Just a sec!" Cooper pulls out the bottle of acid, unscrews the dropper, and dumps what's left of the contents onto the car's front tire. Then he's in action again, running full bore, his chest on fire as he struggles for breath.

The five-foot wall that was easy to scale on the way in is almost too much for him, and he wastes precious seconds dragging himself over the top. He drops to the ground on the other side and scrambles across the highway into the woods in search of his bike. Thirty seconds later, he's off, pedaling down the road with the kind of energy he never dreamed he had left.

He pulls the phone from his pocket and checks the time. It's 11:52—oh, no! He was supposed to be at school more than twenty minutes ago! He had no idea burglary was so time-consuming.

Roddy appears on the GX-4000's screen. "Is there a problem, Coopervega?"

"I'm late," Cooper gasps. "And I still have to ride all the way back to school. The other kids are going to kill me; Jolie will be mad; Mr. Marchese's going to have a heart attack."

"Chillax, my dearest friend," the ghost soothes. "Thou hast accomplished a great deed this day."

"A great deed for *you*," Cooper shoots back in a strained voice as he pedals harder to tackle a steep hill. "But I'm dead meat."

"Speak not so lightly of death," Roddy advises. "Late thou may be. Yet thou shalt be there when the curtain riseth, alive and well. Fear not! Thy troubles are at an end."

In the distance, a car engine sounds on the road behind them, and Cooper veers over to the shoulder to let it pass. A quick glance behind, however, reveals that passing is not what this driver has in mind. A silver Rolls-Royce roars along the highway, gaining fast.

Wolfson's Rolls-Royce.

CHAPTER TWENTY-FIVE
PLACES, EVERYBODY

"It's The Wolf!" Cooper rasps, pedaling like mad.

The bike speeds up, but Cooper knows it's a lost cause. No bicycle can outrun a car.

The Rolls closes the gap quickly, pulling even with the bike. At the wheel is the security guard from the museum. In the passenger seat is Mr. Wolfson himself.

The security man gives a warning honk and motions for Cooper to pull over and stop.

Suddenly, there's a loud *boom* as the car's right front tire blows out. The Rolls goes down on one rim with a screech and a shower of sparks. The driver wrestles the wheel for control and brings the crippled automobile to a lurching halt three inches from the ditch.

Cooper pedals on, streaking away fast as relief supplies his aching body with renewed strength.

"What happened, Coopervega?"

Cooper allows himself a strained smile. "I might have been too hard on your dad's legacy. Maybe his acid works better than I thought."

He risks another look over his shoulder. Far behind him, the two occupants are out of the car, investigating the damage. The angry billionaire is talking on his cell phone.

The ride is long and grueling. Soon, Cooper is so sweaty that he barely trusts himself to handle the GX-4000, which is the only source of time updates—12:04 . . . 12:17 . . . 12:33. The return trip is taking even longer than he thought because the school is atop one of Stratford's original three hills, which means the path ahead is mostly rising. Call time was more than an hour ago. He can only imagine what must be going on in the gym. You can have *Romeo and Juliet* without Second Watchman. Without Romeo, you're finished.

Being Whatshisface is the best he can hope for now. What the cast and crew are probably calling him is a lot worse than that. And whatever chances he might have had with Jolie are circling the bowl.

He checks the phone again: 12:41. Nineteen minutes to curtain. If he somehow gets there in time, he'll still need costume and makeup—for sure, he's sweating too much for any powder to sop it up. And even then, it'll take until act 4 for him to catch his breath. Maybe Brock's nasal twang would be better than a soundless whisper.

Roddy provides encouragement through the earbud. "Treadle strong, Coopervega! Thou shalt win the day!"

"Don't bother!" Cooper pants miserably. "We're too far away. It would take a miracle to get us to school in time!"

All at once, a car drives through the intersection ahead, screeches to a halt, and reverses to block their path. Silently, the window retracts to reveal Veronica in the passenger seat, Chad at the wheel.

"Get in the car!" she shrieks.

"I have to get to school!" he shouts back.

"We know that! Half the town's looking for you! Get in the car!"

Abandoning the bike against a mailbox, Cooper hurls himself into the back and lies there, hugging the knapsack with the precious manuscript inside.

"You are some wacky kid," Chad comments, roaring into a U-turn.

Veronica is already on the phone. "Call off the search party. We've got him . . . Yeah, he's okay, if you don't count stupid. We'll meet you at the school. Bye, Mom."

"Mom?" Cooper echoes in horror. "How does she know about this?"

"When you didn't show up, Mr. Marchese called the house. Mom and Dad are freaking out. Dad was *this* close to bringing in the Army Rangers. Way to go, Cooper. If this is a cry for attention, mission accomplished."

Cooper holds his head. Now his parents are upset. This day is like poison ivy—every time you think the worst is over, another body part starts to itch. And the craziest thing is he'll never be able to explain that all this is *their* fault.

They're the ones who bought him a phone with a hitch-hiker in it!

By the time they reach the school, the parking lot is packed with cars. Curtain time is eight minutes away, and the show is a sellout. Chad wheels them along the front drive and Cooper leaps out to find himself in the arms of his tearful mother.

"Later, Mom. I've got to get into costume!"

His father isn't as emotional. "There'd better be an explanation, mister!"

And there is—but not one that would make any sense.

He's rescued by—of all people—Mr. Marchese. The director's face is so lacking in color that he doesn't appear to have lips. His mouth is just a narrow horizontal slash. He's covered in even more perspiration than Cooper, who has biked halfway up a mountain. And his words are just as breathless.

"I know you must have a lot of questions for your son right now," he tells the Vegas, "but you'll have to wait. I need my actor." He grabs Cooper by the wrist and starts towing him into the building.

"Mr. Marchese," Cooper manages, "I'm so sorry—"

"I don't want to hear it," the teacher cuts in. "Save your breath. You're going to need it onstage. Lucky for you, we're holding the curtain a few extra minutes. Mr. Wolfson is running late. He had car trouble."

Right. Maybe he got sixteenth-century acid on his tire. There's a lot of that going around.

Backstage, the cast is frantic. They take in Cooper's last-minute arrival, some with relief, most with hostility.

"Dude—we were worried about you!" Aiden calls as Cooper rushes past.

But the worst is facing Jolie. She regards him with a combination of accusation and hurt. "I honestly believed drama was important to you! I honestly thought you *cared*!"

"I *do*—"

Before Cooper can draft some kind of explanation, Mr. Marchese shoves him into the locker room. "Get changed," the director orders. "I'll tell makeup you're on your way."

The heavy door closes, and Cooper finds himself alone once more.

"Hark, Coopervega," comes Roddy's voice through the earbud. "Did I not guarantee thou wouldst be here to perform thy part?"

"Is that what you get out of all this?" Cooper explodes. "That everything's hunky-dory? My parents are mad; the teachers are mad; the kids are mad; Jolie hates my guts."

"Thou shalt win her over with thy Romeo," Roddy promises.

"I'm sweaty and dirty. I smell like a hog. I don't know how she's going to stand beside me on the stage, much less decide she likes me again." Cooper throws off his clammy, dusty clothes and struggles into the tights and tunic of Romeo Montague. The backpack and its precious cargo he stashes inside locker 82—for 1582, the year Roddy was born. "I'll talk to you after the play." He removes the earbud and places it on the shelf above the bag.

That leaves only the phone. He has to find a place to stash it so that Roddy can see his masterpiece being performed. He rushes out of the locker room.

"Makeup!" Mr. Marchese orders, beckoning.

Cooper dashes onto the stage. The curtain is down, but he can hear the excited buzz of the crowd on the other side. He locates a spot in the wings just out of the audience's view. The papier-mâché Verona city wall has a small tear in it, and he inserts the GX-4000 into the slit and taps it down so that only the corner with the camera lens sticks out. "Enjoy the show, buddy," he whispers, and then runs offstage to get his makeup on.

It's a rush job, but at least he'll be able to go on with a clean face. The only problem reflected in the mirror is his eyes, which are wide, staring, and somewhat bloodshot—not very Romeo-like. Oh, well; they probably won't notice in the last row.

Mr. Marchese appears over his shoulder. "Mr. Wolfson just arrived. Places, everybody. Curtain in sixty seconds."

The members of the chorus rush out onto the stage. There's an enthusiastic round of applause as the curtain rises. The narrator speaks the opening lines of the play:

"Two households, both alike in dignity . . ."

The words—spoken endlessly in rehearsal—light a fire under the cast. This time it counts for real.

Romeo and Juliet is on!

Crew members bustle around the wings, tweaking lights and ensuring that the staging goes as planned. Actors take their positions for entrances and exits. As Cooper steps onstage for Romeo's first appearance, he checks the Verona city wall to make sure the GX-4000's camera is still peeking out at the stage. He delivers Romeo's first line: *"Is the day so young?"*

As soon as the question is out of his mouth, the horrors of the morning melt away and he's playing the role he's rehearsed so well—in private with Roddy and later with the entire cast.

A glance across the footlights throws him for a loop, and he almost chokes on his next speech. It's The Wolf—front row center—glaring up at him.

He recognizes me! Of course he does! It was broad daylight and the Rolls-Royce was maybe four feet away . . .

By this time, Mr. Wolfson has surely examined the secret gallery. He knows exactly what's missing.

And I'm the guy who asked about Barnabas and Ursula *on the field trip . . .*

With great effort, Cooper forces his mind back to his role and soldiers on. As mad as The Wolf may be, he's watching the play, not shutting it down.

Maybe if we give him a good show, he'll be in a forgiving mood.

Fat chance. Now that he's been robbed of a priceless manuscript, who knows what Somerset Wolfson might do?

The Vegas are seated a few rows behind The Wolf. Cooper's mom is doing her best to enjoy the play, but his dad just looks ticked off. No way is he going to let a timeless classic distract him from the beef he has with his son. As for Veronica, if she's glanced in the general direction of the stage so far, it's news to Cooper. She and Chad are a few rows away, snuggling.

Who do they think they are—Romeo and Juliet?

Next to Chad sits his brother, Brock. If anybody in the gym looks nastier and more miserable than The Wolf, it's the former Romeo with the two black eyes. It can't be easy for him to sit there, anticipating love scenes between his girl and Whatshisface.

Brock would be thrilled to learn that Jolie has washed her hands of Cooper—her and everybody else in the seventh grade. But there's no way for him to know that right now. If they do a good acting job, they can still give the big jerk cramps.

When Cooper heads offstage for Juliet's scene with Lady Capulet, Mr. Marchese is there to greet him with a slap on the back. "Outstanding!" the director raves, bright pink and hyperexcited. "I'm sorry I was hard on you, but you're really knocking it out of the park. Great job!"

That's when Cooper starts to notice that the eyes on him

aren't quite so hostile anymore. Could it be that he's starting to turn this around?

Jolie will be the real test of that.

Their first scene together is the Capulets' ball, where they're supposed to fall in love at first sight. Roddy believes that, in spite of everything, she'll forgive him. Then again, Roddy thinks the most beautiful color in the modern world is school-bus yellow.

Romeo comes up behind Juliet, and Cooper delivers his first words to her: *"If I profane with my unworthiest hand . . ."*

She faces him, shy eyes shining. At minimum, it looks like she doesn't want to punch him out anymore. That's better than nothing. Is she forgiving him or just acting? It's impossible to tell.

One thing seems clear. If he's going to win her over, it'll have to be with his performance.

Luckily, there's no better play for exactly this situation than *Romeo and Juliet.* Cooper pours every ounce of sincerity he can muster into Romeo's romancing. He's been good before, but tonight he's on a whole new level. The audience has no way of knowing that the overpowering emotion of his acting has nothing to do with the story and everything to do with the fact that he messed up so badly, and desperately wants to fix things with Jolie.

The crowd watches, spellbound by the famous star-crossed lovers. Cooper ratchets up the passion in the balcony scene. Jolie's right there with him, matching his ardor. The question remains: Is it real or is it pure theater?

If it means nothing more than that she's stopped hating him, he'll settle for it. It feels fantastic.

The audience is totally into it. They gasp in shock when Tybalt accidentally kills Mercutio, and cry out in horror when the vengeful Romeo kills Tybalt.

At intermission, the entire seventh grade is pumped. Even during the very best of their dress rehearsals, the performance was never this inspired. The actors are feeding off the energy of the audience, flushed with growing triumph. If this keeps up, *Romeo and Juliet* is going to be an epic blockbuster.

Mr. Marchese's lips are back, and so is the color in his cheeks, which are very nearly purple. An hour ago, he was facing the disaster of having to cancel the whole event due to no Romeo, round two. Now he's looking to go down as the greatest director the Shakespeare program has ever had.

His eyes are alight as he gathers the cast and crew to greet "a very special visitor."

A jolt of electricity shoots up Cooper's spine.

It's The Wolf.

CHAPTER TWENTY-SIX
THIS ONE'S FOR YOU

The billionaire is already applauding them as he ascends the backstage steps. "Excellent work, everyone. I kept checking my program to confirm that I wasn't watching the Royal Shakespeare Company itself."

As The Wolf goes on about how much he's enjoying the show, Cooper suddenly realizes that the man is scanning faces, one by one, searching for somebody.

Searching for me!

"Ah—Romeo." The dark eyes lock on Cooper. "Your performance has moved me. I look forward to the second half—*and* the aftermath."

When Mr. Wolfson has returned to his seat, the entire grade swarms Cooper. It's tradition that The Wolf never singles any one performer out. This proves that Cooper's Romeo is truly extraordinary.

Cooper knows better. By "aftermath," the billionaire is telling him that a confrontation is coming up—probably one where The Wolf holds a dagger to Cooper's head and says, "Give me back my manuscript or else."

Cooper has the rest of the play—about an hour—to figure out what he's going to do. What will he say? What will he give back, if anything? Can he work up the guts to tell Somerset Wolfson the plain truth: *That manuscript doesn't belong to you.* And how can he ever explain why?

As the cast returns to the stage, Cooper catches sight of Jolie looking at him. Tentatively—hopefully—he casts a smile in her direction, but she's already turned away.

Oh, well, he thinks, setting his jaw. It's not like she's the biggest of his problems at the moment. He's doing this for Roddy, and he's going to see it through.

In the second half, the actors continue to outdo themselves, and the performance soars. By this time, The Wolf has given up any pretense of watching *Romeo and Juliet.* He's focused on Cooper, staring him down. As Romeo crosses the stage, the smoldering dark eyes follow.

Having a billionaire plotting against you is pretty scary, so Cooper blocks it out of his mind by concentrating on Roddy. How must it feel for the ghost to see his long-lost words come to life before him? And now that the part Roddy wrote is done, and Shakespeare's tragic conclusion is starting to build, what thoughts are going through his Elizabethan head?

Shakespeare may have ripped off the work of a thirteen-year-old printer's apprentice, but when it came to orchestrating a real downer ending, nobody could touch him. What began as love at first sight is soon spiraling out of control into disaster. Although Cooper has rehearsed this many times, tonight it's as if he's experiencing the tragedy for real. One by one, the plot twists unfold, each dragging Romeo and Juliet closer to the point where they take their own lives. When he comes upon her lifeless body in the Capulet family crypt, his grief is genuine. He cries—Cooper *never* cries!—and only part of it is acting.

The flask of poison that he drinks is filled with water, but it tastes bitter and lethal. And when he drops to the stage, it's more than just a fall. It feels like death.

At last, Cooper and Jolie lie side by side in the crypt, as the narrator delivers the closing lines of the play:

> *"For never was a story of more woe*
> *Than this of Juliet and her Romeo."*

Waves of thunderous applause wash over the stage. Cooper's eyes are closed, so he isn't sure exactly when the curtain comes down until Aiden drags him and Jolie to their feet. "Dudes!" he crows. "You *killed* the death scene! You *owned*!"

For the first time since the play began, Jolie meets Cooper's eyes, as herself, not as Juliet. "You were fantastic!"

"Because of you—" he tries to reply. But cast and crew are already stampeding in from the wings, wild with excitement, and it's impossible to communicate.

So she communicates in a better way. She leans forward and kisses him softly on the cheek.

The only words to describe it come from Roddy: *How now!*

Cooper gets to enjoy the thrill for about three seconds. The curtain goes up to reveal a standing ovation of parents, neighbors, and friends. Only one chair lacks a cheering audience member in front of it, and it's as glaringly obvious as a missing tooth. Front row, center.

The Wolf is gone.

No, not gone. There he is, at the back of the gym, in front of the far doors, ushering in two uniformed policemen.

Fear jolts through Cooper, but he reminds himself that he has no right to be surprised. How does he expect the rich and powerful to deal with people who steal from them?

I'm going to be arrested in front of the whole town—including my own parents!

He wrestles his rising panic under control. There's no way to change what's about to happen to him. All he can do is follow through on his original plan.

As the rousing curtain calls go on, Cooper slips off the stage.

"Take another bow!" Mr. Marchese urges. "You saved our play! You deserve this more than anybody!"

Cooper ignores him, dashing through the wings to the locker room and number 82. He pulls the manuscript out of his bag, jams the earbud into his ear, and rushes back onto the stage. As he passes the Verona city wall, he plucks the GX-4000 out of the crack and jams it in the belt of his tunic.

"Bravo!" The ghost's voice is husky with emotion. "The ending might have been cheerier, but that was beyond thy control."

"Pay attention, Roddy," Cooper intones. "This one's for you."

The applause swells once again as the triumphant Romeo strides to center stage. He holds up a hand for order, and the audience quiets down.

"Thank you for coming to our play," he announces. "And a special thanks to Mr. Wolfson for making it all possible."

The Wolf does a very bad job of concealing his rage, as he acknowledges his ovation with a *you're welcome* wave.

Cooper draws a deep breath and swallows hard. This is it!

"I want to tell you about the *real* play. It wasn't called *Romeo and Juliet* back then. It was called *Barnabas and Ursula*. And the reason I know about it is because I have it right here." He holds up Roddy's manuscript, fanning it out to give the audience a view of the handwritten pages.

An impressed "Oooooh" comes from the seats. Cooper is encouraged that the crowd is with him, but he doesn't let it go to his head. He hasn't hit them with the weird part yet.

"Coopervega"—the ghost's tone is bewildered—"what sayest thou?"

Cooper ignores him. "The thing is," he goes on, *"Barnabas and Ursula* wasn't written by William Shakespeare. It was written by a thirteen-year-old printer's apprentice named Roderick Northrop. In 1596, before the play was done, Roddy died of the plague. The unfinished manuscript was discovered under Roddy's mattress by Shakespeare, who was at the shop because he was having one of his own plays printed there. So he stole *Barnabas and Ursula,* changed the names to Romeo and Juliet, and wrote his own ending."

A confused murmur rises up in the gym. To the audience, this started as a fun fact about the play they just watched. But now this kid seems to be telling them that William Shakespeare didn't write *Romeo and Juliet.* Not only that, but he *ripped it off*—from a dead thirteen-year-old, no less. What kind of crazy story is that?

The Vegas are staring at their son in openmouthed amazement. Even Veronica has torn her eyes from Chad to gawk at her brother. Brock looks completely lost behind his bandage. None of this was part of the script when *he* was Romeo. Only the presence of the two cops is keeping The Wolf from leaping onto the stage and duct-taping Cooper's mouth shut.

"Cooper!" Mr. Marchese hisses. "What's this about?"

Cooper forges on. He has to make his point while he still

has everybody's attention. "Even though Shakespeare gave the play a tragic ending, it was always Roddy's plan for Barnabas and Ursula to live happily ever after. He didn't survive to write the last two lines, but here's what they were going to be."

He reveals the conclusion the ghost told him he'd had in mind:

> *"No greater tale of joy could come to pass*
> *Than this of Ursula and her Barnabas.*

"Some of you might have wanted to see that happy ending," Cooper continues, "and some of you might think the sad one is better. But the good parts—the stuff that makes this the greatest love story ever—that was all Roddy. He died before he could get credit for his work, but I think he deserves a big thank-you from all of us."

Dead silence greets this statement. Undaunted, Cooper tucks the manuscript under his arm and begins to clap. Those few seconds—when he's the only one—are the loneliest of his entire life.

He hears a second pair of hands, and Jolie steps up to stand with him. With Romeo and Juliet both on board, the entire cast and crew bursts into applause. Slowly, like ripples crossing a pond, the audience joins in until the ovation is deafening—far too loud for anyone to hear the click.

What happens next will never be forgotten in the town of Stratford, even though no two people saw exactly the same thing, and many saw nothing at all.

A shimmering form rises above the lead actors on the stage. A trick of the light, perhaps? The power of suggestion? A cloud of smoke from an overheated spotlight?

Or, some say, the slender silhouette of a young teenage boy, taking an elaborate bow.

The figure shifts, stretching to envelop the manuscript in Cooper's arms. The glittering mass begins to spin, losing its shape as it picks up speed.

With a loud pop, a footlight blows. High above, two spotlights short-circuit in a shower of sparks. *Boom!* The main lighting array goes off like a fireworks display. For an instant, the stage is as bright as high noon. Then it's over, leaving actors and spectators alike squinting into the gloom, jittery with alarm.

A moment later, the regular gym lights come on. Smoke from the burst lighting hangs heavy in the air. The cast and crew of *Romeo and Juliet* stand motionless on the stage, Cooper at the front. The mysterious shimmering cloud is gone.

Gone too is the manuscript of *Barnabas and Ursula*.

CHAPTER TWENTY-SEVEN
UNDER ARREST

That day, Cooper becomes the first Romeo ever to be arrested after a performance of *Romeo and Juliet*. Within thirty seconds of the gym lights coming back on, he's flanked by the two cops and marched off the stage. Veronica almost gets arrested with him for trying to wrestle her brother away from the officers. Cooper is amazed. Who knew she even liked him, much less that she'd be willing to take on armed policemen to keep him out of custody?

He ends up in the principal's office, one on one with The Wolf, while the Vegas wait outside. The cops are in the gym, searching the backstage area and locker room for the missing manuscript.

"All right, kid. Where is it?" the billionaire demands.

"I don't know," Cooper replies honestly. "You saw what happened. Everybody did."

"I saw some sleight-of-hand trick," The Wolf acknowledges. "The kind of misdirection tactic every third-rate magician learns on day one."

"Seriously?" Cooper challenges him. "You think I rigged all those lights to blow just to give me a few seconds to stash the manuscript in a secret hiding place? Do you really think I know how to do that?"

The dark eyes are nearly black now. "You knew how to break into my museum—and you knew exactly what to steal."

Cooper flushes, shamefaced. "I admit that. I'll pay for whatever damage I did. But I can't tell you where the manuscript is now, because I don't know. It was under my arm when the lights went out. When they came back on, it was gone."

"Pay for the damage," Mr. Wolfson snorts bitterly. "A priceless manuscript is missing. Who pays for that?"

"Sorry," Cooper mumbles. He can't tell the billionaire the truth: He didn't steal *Barnabas and Ursula*; he restored it to its rightful owner. On the other hand, The Wolf didn't steal it either. He wasn't the one who pulled it out from under the mattress of a poor, dead apprentice. Shakespeare himself did that long before this man was even born.

Still, Mr. Wolfson probably paid a lot to buy it. "Well, at least you'll get the insurance money, right?" Cooper ventures.

The Wolf is tight-lipped. "The manuscript isn't insured."

Cooper is stunned. "How come? Weren't you worried that something might happen to it? Something *did* happen to it!"

The billionaire looks away.

All at once, Cooper has the answer. "You never insured it

because you couldn't admit it existed in the first place! It's the only handwritten Shakespeare manuscript in the world. There's just one problem—it's in the wrong handwriting! It's proof that Shakespeare ripped off *Romeo and Juliet*. And if he stole that, who knows what else he stole? You've got a whole museum of stuff that would be worthless if Shakespeare turned out to be a fraud."

The Wolf draws his shoulders up in anger. "The Bard of Avon is not a fraud! Copyists rewrote plays by hand all the time back then. How else could the actors learn their lines?"

"Yeah, but those copyists didn't change the names of the characters and move the setting to another city," Cooper retorts. "Or put 'by Roderick Northrop' at the top."

"Roderick Northrop!" the billionaire sneers. "Where did you get *that* tall tale? My researchers tell me there might have been as many as three thousand Roderick Northrops in England around that time."

"How many of them worked in the very same place where Shakespeare had his printing done?"

Mr. Wolfson grimaces. "That story is patently absurd. Yes, there was a boy of that name apprenticed to the shop of Mannering and Brown. So what? As if any thirteen-year-old would be capable of creating the glory that is *Romeo and Juliet*."

"Hey!" A tsunami of irritation washes over Cooper. "You can say bad things about me, but lay off Roddy Northrop. He was a good writer—*better* than Shakespeare. And if he'd lived to write the ending, you can bet that it wouldn't have been such a bummer!"

The billionaire frowns disapprovingly. "You talk about this long-dead boy as if he's a personal friend of yours."

Cooper almost says, *Maybe he is*, but bites his lip instead. Why give this powerful man any more ammunition against him?

There hasn't been a peep out of Roddy since the end of the play. True, that was only forty-five minutes ago. But forty-five minutes of silence isn't Roddy's style. Three minutes is a stretch for him. Cooper isn't quite ready to let himself think about what this might mean.

His reverie is interrupted by the return of the two police officers.

"Sorry, Mr. Wolfson," the older cop offers. "The search turned up nothing. I don't know where your property is, but it's not here."

"I see," the billionaire rumbles.

"I suggest we take the kid in for questioning," the other goes on. "Could be he passed the manuscript off to an accomplice when the lights went out. We'll need a detailed description of the missing article and a photograph, if you've got one. Also, an estimate of the value."

There's a long silence from Stratford's leading citizen. At last, he speaks. "Officers, I hope you'll forgive me. This has been one big misunderstanding. Nothing is missing. It was all part of the truly remarkable performance these young people put on today."

The older cop is unconvinced. "What about the break-in at your museum this morning?"

"Vandalism," the billionaire assures him. "An unrelated incident."

"You said an important manuscript was stolen—"

"Merely misplaced. I just heard from my people. We were mistaken. Everything is where it should be."

It's pretty obvious that the officers don't believe him. On the other hand, he's Somerset Wolfson. No one in Stratford will call him a liar—not even the police.

"You're dropping all charges, then?" the older cop asks him.

"Of course," replies The Wolf, nearly choking on the words.

As the officers exit, Cooper realizes how lucky he is to be off the hook. Too well he understands that, if *Barnabas and Ursula* wasn't a threat to Shakespeare's almighty reputation, he would still be under arrest right now.

"Thank you for clearing my name," he says.

The billionaire scowls. "Your name isn't clear with me. I'm watching you, kid, and I can afford a lot of eyes to help me. If I ever get word that my manuscript is out there somewhere, you can expect all the trouble you dodged today."

"You won't," Cooper promises. He has no way of knowing this. Yet somehow in his heart, he is certain that *Barnabas and Ursula* is safe in the hands of its author.

Without another word, Somerset Wolfson gets up and walks quietly out of the room, brushing right past the Vegas and Veronica, who are waiting in the outer office.

Before rushing to rejoin his anxious family, Cooper can't resist pulling the GX-4000 out of his pocket and checking for Roddy.

A single text message awaits him—time: 3:11 p.m., precisely the moment the ghost and the manuscript disappeared. Holding the phone in trembling hands, Cooper reads it.

I shall never forget thee.

CHAPTER TWENTY-EIGHT
A GRAY LIE

The ride home is only half a mile, but the Vegas manage to pack a lot of interrogation into it. What happened at the end of the play? What was that speech accusing Shakespeare of stealing *Romeo and Juliet* from a dead kid?

"It was part of the show," Cooper tells them. Not a white lie, exactly, but at least a gray one. Anyway, The Wolf pretty much implied that to the cops, and no one would ever challenge a statement from him.

"It didn't seem like it," Mrs. Vega counters.

"A million schools put on *Romeo and Juliet*," Cooper reasons. "We wanted to make ours a little different. You know, memorable."

"I'm never going to forget it," puts in Veronica, giving Cooper a sharp elbow.

"Seriously," Cooper persists. "That manuscript—it was a prop."

"So how come Mr. Wolfson tried to have you arrested?" Captain Vega demands.

Cooper shrugs. "He didn't understand at first—when it

comes to Shakespeare, the guy has no sense of humor. Once I explained it to him, everything was okay. You saw."

Mrs. Vega won't let it go. "But what happened onstage at the very end? There was a cloud—but it looked almost like a person."

"You imagined it, Mom. The lighting went crazy right before it blew."

"I saw it too," Cooper's father agrees with her.

"Same," Veronica adds, "and that was definitely *before* the lights went kablooey."

"Fine," Cooper says in exasperation. "What do you want me to tell you? It was the ghost of Roderick Northrop coming back to take his manuscript and claim credit for the play Shakespeare stole. Does that make more sense? The entire town of Stratford saw the ghost of a thirteen-year-old kid. When's your next transfer, Dad? We've got to get out of this place before we end up nuts too."

Captain Vega snorts. "I suppose you think you're funny. You want to talk about ghosts? Show me the ghost who made off with our toilet plunger."

The family laughs, and Cooper sinks back into the seat, toying with the idea that he might just get away with this. The Vegas seem satisfied, and The Wolf sure isn't going to spill the beans.

Still, he wonders—how do you convince an entire gym full of people that they didn't really see what they saw?

FAULTY WIRING DISRUPTS TRIUMPHANT MIDDLE SCHOOL PLAY

The Stratford Globe, Local News

School board officials confirm that faulty wiring was to blame for the failure of the lighting array during Stratford Middle School's otherwise flawless production of Shakespeare's Romeo and Juliet.

The incident occurred during the curtain call. The exploding bulbs created such a display that some observers reported that their eyes were playing tricks on them. "Rapid-fire flashes of multicolored light often create optical illusions," commented Somerset Wolfson, sponsor of the annual event. Mr. Wolfson's love of Shakespeare has been legendary in town history.

In an unrelated story, the nationally renowned Wolfson Shakespeare Collection will be closed until further notice for maintenance and minor repairs.

EPILOGUE

The GX-4000 isn't buggy anymore. It powers down when Cooper tells it to, and opens only the apps he touches. The camera takes perfect pictures without a hint of distortion. The hype is true. It really is the most advanced smartphone on the market.

Cooper liked it better before.

It's nothing against the phone, obviously. He misses Roddy with a longing that's almost painful. It was just a couple of months, but during that time, the ghost was more than his one friend. Thanks to the earbud, Roddy was literally inside Cooper's head. It was like having a roommate in your brain. And while all roommates get on each other's nerves here and there, the word *close* doesn't begin to describe what they shared. It's an empty space Cooper knows he'll never be able to fill.

He'd give almost anything to hear another "How now, Coopervega," or one more of Roddy's lectures about what "Methinks . . ." But he knows that Roddy and his manuscript are finally in the place they're supposed to be—wherever that is.

It was the bow that did it, Cooper decides—the spectacular soaring bow where Roddy finally received acclaim for the work of genius he wrote all those years ago.

It's funny—Cooper has become famous in Stratford as the star of *Romeo and Juliet* and its stunning post-ending. He has friends now. Even Brock remembers his name most of the time. And he has a girlfriend—Roddy never got his Ursula, but he sure was right about Jolie. But Cooper's greatest achievement is one he can never tell anyone about—not even Jolie.

How many seventh graders can figure out a way to finish the quest of a sixteenth-century ghost seeking to right a wrong he never knew about, because the injustice happened after his death?

It's the kind of thing you can only hug to yourself, smiling into the darkness as you fall asleep at night.

Not every Whatshisface can accomplish something like that.

ABOUT THE AUTHOR

Gordon Korman is the #1 bestselling author of four books in The 39 Clues series as well as eight books in his Swindle series: *Swindle, Zoobreak, Framed, Showoff, Hideout, Jackpot, Unleashed,* and *Jingle.* His other books include *This Can't Be Happening at Macdonald Hall!* (published when he was fourteen); *The Toilet Paper Tigers; Radio Fifth Grade; Ungifted; Schooled; Slacker; Restart;* the trilogies The Hypnotists, Island, Everest, Dive, Kidnapped, and Titanic; and the series On the Run. He lives in New York with his family and can be found on the Web at gordonkorman.com.

DISCOVER
THESE FANTASTIC READS BY
GORDON KORMAN!

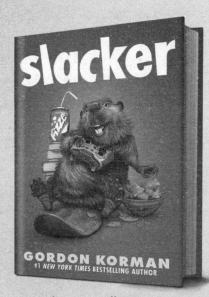

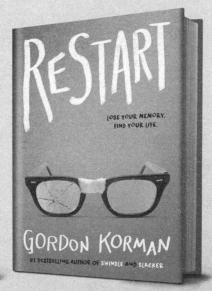

How does an all-star slacker end up achieving more than any overachiever could ever imagine?

After losing his memory, it's not only a question of who Chase is—it's a question of who he was... and who he's going to be.

scholastic.com